The
Barin Field
MURDER

The
Barin Field
MURDER

Randolph Crew

ARTEC

The Barin Field Murder

Book Three in the *Four Seasons Series*
A Nate and Superman Cozy Murder Mystery
with Detective Dan Lewis

Copyright © 2025 by Randolph Crew
Published by Artec Publishing
ISBN#: 978-0-9651430-5-9
Library of Congress Control Number: 2025904196

This novel is a work of fiction. Except as noted in the Author's Preface, names, characters, places, and incidents are either the product of the author's imagination or are used fictitiously. Any resemblance to actual events or persons, living or dead, is entirely coincidental and beyond the author's or publisher's intent.

Edited by Julianne Epps
Copy edited by Wendy Chorot
Cover design by Margarita Castaño
Interior design by Roseanna White Designs
Map created by O'Neill & Clark
Aircraft illustrations by Brian Argo and Dave Wommer
Printed in the United States of America
First paperback edition: April, 2025
First Kindle edition: April, 2025

Novels by Randolph Crew

The Gulf Shores Murder
The Barin Field Murder

The Christmas Tree Corpse
The Trick-or-Treat Corpse

A Killing Shadow
One-Way Mission

To the memory of my father, Colonel Erskine B. Crew, a NAVCAD student pilot (Marine Option), who trained at Barin Field in 1942, and then as a Marine Second Lieutenant, served as a Fighter Pilot Instructor at Barin Field in 1944. He flew training flights out of Barin when it was known as "Bloody Barin" due to all the training accidents and pilot deaths—forty deaths in two years.

And to the memory of my mother, Martha Hawke Crew, who tolerated and loved her Marine fighter-pilot husband and his rowdy Marine friends for fifty-seven years, including three wars and multiple deployments. My mother exemplified the words from the last line of John Milton's 1651 epic sonnet about patience: "They also serve who only stand and wait."

"The saddest thing in life and the hardest to live through, is the knowledge that there is someone you love very much whom you cannot save from suffering."
Agatha Christie

ACKNOWLEDGEMENTS

I thank Paul Leonard of the Foley Public Library Local History and Genealogy Collections Department for his information on Foley and Barin Field history. Also extremely helpful were LaDonna Hinesley and Guy Busby of the Foley Marketing Department and Sandy Russell of the Foley Museum and Archives Board.

I also want to thank Julianne Epps for the story edit and critique; Charlotte Ainsworth for her fearless first-draft editing and critique; Wendy Chorot for the final edit; Jake Nowland, the "Happy Sailor," for his information on gunnery training in the '50s; David Schwartz and Larry Taylor for their information on what it was like when they flew gunnery training flights; Larry Grandy for his advice on aircraft accident investigations; and Justin Clark for his website design, map illustration, and guidance in the baffling world of computers.

In my efforts to make this novel both gripping fiction

and, at the same time, historically accurate in time and place, I wanted to portray Pensacola and Foley in 1956 accurately and fairly. Still, if I've made mistakes, they are entirely my own and should not reflect on the people who helped me. I sincerely thank them all.

PREFACE

Pensacola, Barin Field, and Foley; Then and Now.

As you can tell from my bio, I have a special bond with Pensacola, Florida. Not only was I born there, but I lived there from 1948 to 1950 when my father was stationed there again, and I started first grade there. In this book, I wanted to share the 1950s Pensacola with you so you will find venues mentioned in the book that are still around and some that aren't.

For example, the **L&N train depot** in Pensacola is still there but is now the reception area for the Crowne Plaza Pensacola Grand Hotel. The **San Carlos Hotel**, known affectionately as the "Gray Lady of Palafox," is no longer there. The **Saenger Theatre** is still on Palafox Place and has been since 1925. The **Pensacola Greyhound Race Track** is now the Pensacola Greyhound Track and Poker Room. The **Pensacola Buggy Works** is no longer there, and unfortunately, neither is **Trader Jon's**, but the Trader Jon's Exhibit is in the Pensacola Museum of History on Jefferson Street. **Ferguson Field** is now Roscoe Field. **Abe's 506 Club** in "The Blocks" is no longer there, but

Five Sisters' Blues Café on the corner of Belmont and DeVilliers is there, serves excellent food, and honors the history of The Blocks. **Captain Ahab's** restaurant is fictional.

The buildings on the campus of N.A.S. Pensacola mentioned in the book, including the **Mustin Beach Officer's Club**, are still there, but building 600, **Mustin Hall**, the former Visiting Officer's Quarters, is inactive, storm-damaged, and in need of repair.

Paradise Beach is still on the western edge of Florida on the way to Barin Field, but the **Paradise Beach Hotel** is no longer there, and the land is now home sites on Paradise Beach Circle.

Barin Field in Foley, Alabama, is still operational as an outlying field for Navy T-6 trainer aircraft from Whiting Field in Milton, Florida. However, none of the barracks and buildings mentioned in the book are still there.

In **Foley**, Highway 98, Laurel Avenue, and Highway 59, McKenzie Street, intersect downtown. When the scene is in Foley, I use the street names, but when the scene is outside the city limits, I use the highway designations. **Foley** was declared an **American WWII Heritage City** in 2024, and a museum of Barin Field and Foley history opened in the old **train depot** in Foley in December of 2024. **Manning Jewelry** on West Laurel Avenue is still there and is run by Glenn Manning, the original owner's son. The USO Club was in the building that is now **The Gift Horse Restaurant**. The **Foley Coffee Shop** on North McKenzie Street is still there. The **Holmes Hospital** building on West Laurel is still there, but the hospital is now a museum, and **Crosby Drug** on the first floor is now a large bookstore called **The Book Exchange**. Stacey's Drug Store on West Laurel is now **Stacey's Olde Tyme Soda Fountain**. The **Hotel Magnolia** on North McKenzie is still there and updated as a beautiful B&B and restaurant. **Billy's Barbeque** and **Dottie's Chicken House** are fictional, but I imagined Dottie's located where the **Dorthy June Booksellers** bookstore on West Orange Avenue is today.

Pensacola, Barin Field, and Foley are great, historic places to have on your bucket list. Come on down and see why this area is still special to me.

Foley, Alabama, 1956

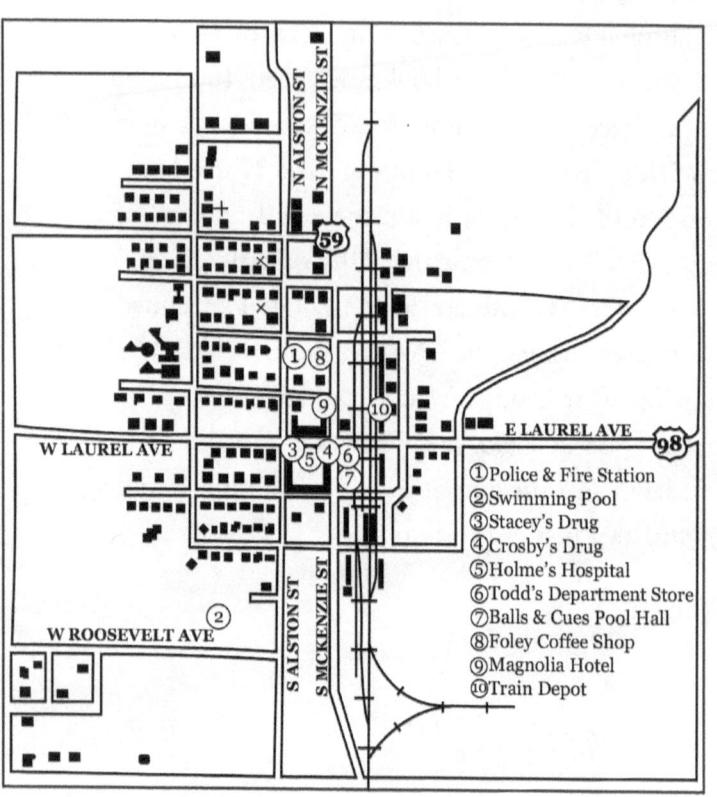

Mullet Point

N ALSTON ST
N MCKENZIE ST

59

S ALSTON ST
S MCKENZIE ST

W LAUREL AVE

E LAUREL AVE — 98

W ROOSEVELT AVE

① Police & Fire Station
② Swimming Pool
③ Stacey's Drug
④ Crosby's Drug
⑤ Holme's Hospital
⑥ Todd's Department Store
⑦ Balls & Cues Pool Hall
⑧ Foley Coffee Shop
⑨ Magnolia Hotel
⑩ Train Depot

Bo

Little Point Clear

St. Andrew's Bay

Fort Morgan

180

N

NW
NE

W — E

SW
SE

S

Sand Island Lighthouse

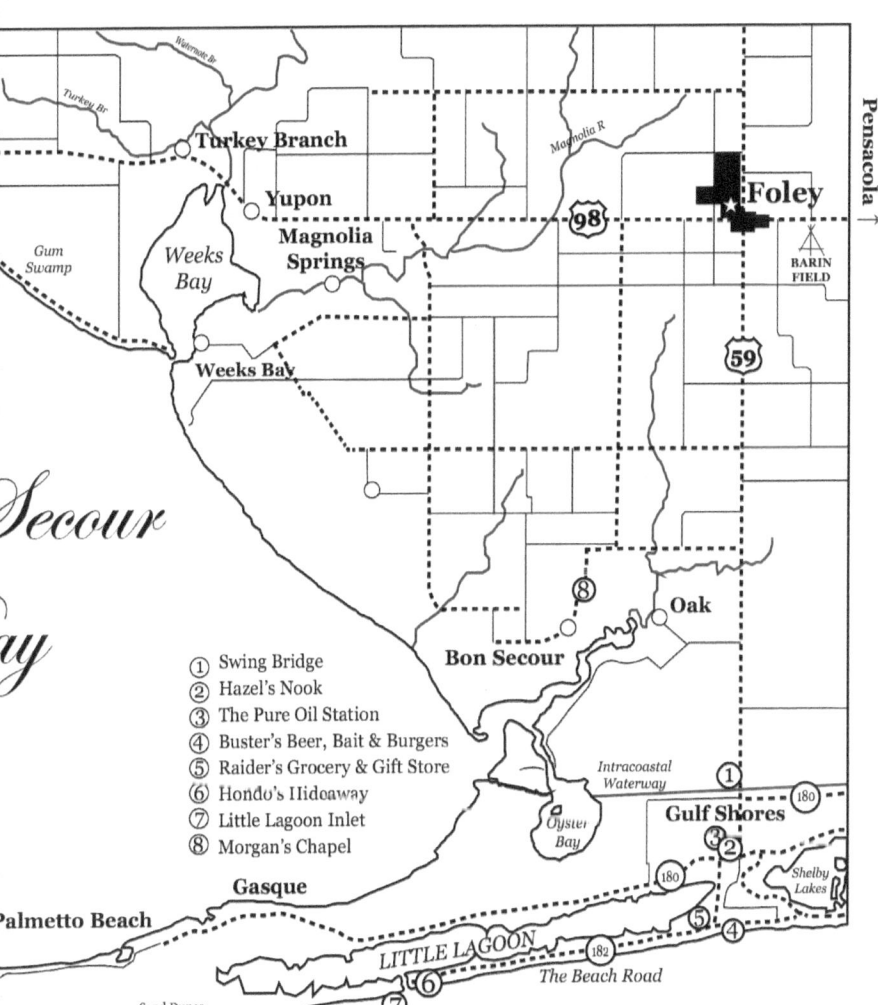

Southern Baldwin County, Alabama, 1956

Pensacola →

Watmott Br

Turkey Br

Turkey Branch

Yupon

Gum Swamp

Weeks Bay

Magnolia Springs

Magnolia R

98

Foley

BARIN FIELD

59

Weeks Bay

Secour

ay

Oak

8

Bon Secour

① Swing Bridge
② Hazel's Nook
③ The Pure Oil Station
④ Buster's Beer, Bait & Burgers
⑤ Raider's Grocery & Gift Store
⑥ Hondo's Hideaway
⑦ Little Lagoon Inlet
⑧ Morgan's Chapel

Intracoastal Waterway

Oyster Bay

① 180

Gulf Shores

③②

Shelby Lakes

Gasque

180

Palmetto Beach

⑤

④

LITTLE LAGOON

182

The Beach Road

Sand Dunes

⑦ ⑥

Naval Aircraft Factory N3N

Description: Two-seat military training biplane
Powerplant: Wright 760-2, 235 horsepower, 7-cylinder air-cooled radial engine
Max speed: 126 mph
Cruising speed: 90 mph
Rate of climb: 800 feet/minute
Service Ceiling: 15,200 feet
Range: 470 miles
Specifications: Wingspan 34 feet, length 25 feet six inches, empty weight 2,090 pounds

North American T-28 Trojan
(Navy models B and C)

Description: Two-seat pilot trainer
Powerplant: Wright R-1820, 9-cylinder air-cooled radial engine with a three-bladed prop
Max speed: 346 mph
Cruising speed: 230mph
Rate of climb: 3,000 feet/minute
Service Ceiling: 37,000 feet
Range: 1,060 miles
Specifications: Wingspan 40 feet six inches, length 32 feet nine inches, empty weight 8,600 pounds
Armament: Two .50 caliber machine gun pods, 1800 pounds of bombs and rockets

Table of Contents

PROLOGUE

My name is Nathan "Nate" Hawke, retired homicide detective, Dallas, Texas. In the spring of 1956, when I was fourteen years old and lived in Sand Hills, North Carolina, our family friend and my mother's co-worker, Detective Dan "Red" Lewis—while dealing with a crime in Sand Hills that led to murder—found himself drawn into another murder investigation in Foley, Alabama. How he solved both simultaneously is his story, so I'll let him tell it, but the one that got all the headlines has become known in Foley and Pensacola, Florida, as the case of *The Barin Field Murder*.

CHAPTER 1
The Accident

Seated in a stuffed armchair in Connie's living room, I opened the Sunday paper and leaned back. Between sips of coffee, I read a story about the Soviet Army threatening Hungary, another about fighting in the Gaza Strip, and another about President Eisenhower's speech on the Farm Bill. But when I got to a story on page three of a naval aviation cadet's death, I did a double-take. I collapsed the paper into my lap and looked across the coffee table.

"Connie!" I said. "The guy in this story is Carl's brother. My old teammate, Carl. Remember? I told you Carl married the richest girl in our school."

"Carl's brother is in the news?" Connie said as she reached over and topped off my coffee, the finishing touch to the Sunday dinners that started a few months into our year-long relationship.

"Yeah, Jeff." I pointed at the paper. "'Cadet Jeff Puckett dies in an aircraft accident.'"

"Air Force cadet?" She pulled her hair back over her ear.

"Naval aviation cadet, NAVCAD. He was in the Navy's flight program at Pensacola, Florida, and was in the gunnery training phase at Barin Field in Foley, Alabama, when he got lost, landed in a farmer's field, and died."

"If he landed safely, that doesn't sound like an accident."

"They're reporting it as an accident in this story, but it says they found the airplane intact and basically undamaged, so it doesn't sound like an accident to me either."

Connie, the widow of a Marine fighter pilot killed in Korea, returned to her end of the sofa opposite Nate, her fourteen-year-old, who closed his Agatha Christie mystery and sat up straight. That boy was all ears when it came to the question of someone's untimely death.

"Well," Connie said, "we know the papers get it wrong sometimes, but what else could it be?"

"Maybe he had a heart attack," Nate said.

"He's a little young for a heart attack, Nate. But I guess it could have been something medical. I don't know, but reading between the lines of this article, I don't think it was a pilot or mechanical kind of accident, and I don't think the reporter is telling all she knows." I folded the paper. "I'll call Carl when I get home and see what's going on."

I finished my coffee, stood tall and stretched, picked up my fedora from the antique side table, and said goodbye to Nate.

"You know, Connie," I said as we walked to the front door. "Jeff has always been the family troublemaker, and Carl's had to cover for him to keep him out of jail. When Carl talked Jeff into this NAVCAD program, he hoped it would give him some discipline and direction in life, and based on Carl's last conversation with me, it worked. It'd be a shame if the program that had turned Jeff around had led to his accidental death." I snugged the fedora over my flat top. "If it was an accident."

"Whoa, Dan," Connie said as she hooked my arm, "why wouldn't it be an accident?"

"Because in the past, Jeff has always been one of those guys drawn to fast women and slow horses. As a result, he spends or bets more than he has and is usually in debt. The last time Jeff came up short, Carl gave him five hundred dollars to keep him from losing his kneecaps to a loan shark. It could be something like that—an unhappy and unpaid loan shark who decided to make Jeff an example to his other customers."

"But how could a loan shark kill a guy in an airplane? Jeff was alone in the airplane, right?"

"According to the newspaper, he was alone, but...ah,

who knows?" I gave Connie a quick hug. "Carl's with a law firm in Pensacola, so he might have some answers. Or he can get some answers. I'll call you after I talk with him."

I placed a long-distance call to Carl that night, but he didn't know anything more than what he'd read in the papers. They called him in to identify the body, but after that, he said the Navy would only say, "We're doing a thorough investigation. We'll get back to you."

So, I said, "Carl, is there any reason to suspect foul play here?"

"Ah, heck, Red, there's always reason to suspect foul play with Jeff. I mean, he'd done really well lately, but he'd still been his usual secretive self. No, I wouldn't rule out foul play."

"Well, what was going on in his life before this accident?"

"Nothing that I know of. Well, nothing like the trouble he had typically been into. I know he was still hanging out at the Pensacola dog track, but I don't think he was betting on the dogs like he did at the track in Charlotte. At least, I don't think he was."

"Have you seen him lately?"

"No, not in weeks. Talked to him a few times; last week was the latest. Heard about his new girlfriend, Betsy, a girl from Foley, Alabama."

"Who were his friends? Have you talked with any of them?"

"Pete Dalton is one of his friends, 'Pistol Pete,' Jeff called him. I talked with Pete yesterday, the day after the accident, but even though he was in the flight of four airplanes with Jeff—Pete was the lead guy in the flight, and Jeff was number four—Pete didn't know Jeff was gone until Pete landed at Barin."

"What were they doing, and when did Pete last see him?"

"They were on a gunnery training flight. An instructor tows a target banner a thousand feet behind his airplane, and four students in T-twenty-eights with fifty-caliber gun pods under their wings attack the banner. I remember Jeff was all excited about starting that phase of training, but I don't know when he was last seen. I didn't ask. But I've got Pete's number if you want to call him. I've tried, but I've never been able to catch him in."

"Yeah, I'll get that number from you before I hang up, but one more question: Do you know the reporter on the scene, this Jamie Lynn Jones?"

"I know of her, but I've never met her."

"Any intel on her?"

"Well, young, I guess you could say, late twenties maybe. Single. Good writer. I've seen her byline many times."

"Local girl?"

"I don't think so. Seems like she came down here from either Birmingham or Atlanta."

"Has she contacted you?"

"No, should she have?"

"Only if she intends to write a follow-up story, which I'm sure she will. This is a story with a lot of unanswered questions, and reporters love staying with a story that will give them more bylines, so I'm sure you'll hear from her."

"Well, when I do, I'll let you know. And thanks for your interest, Red. Glad to have a detective I know and trust to discuss this with."

"I wanna help in any way I can, Carl. Remember, you've been there for me—actually, you *and* Jeff. I haven't forgotten when you guys pulled that gang of Rivertown thugs off me. I still have the scar on my chin from that experience."

"But they got your money."

"Yeah, all five dollars and sixty-five cents."

"Well, you were doing okay when we arrived."

"But I couldn't have lasted much longer, so I'm here for you, Carl. I owe you."

"Heck, Red, you don't owe me. If anything, I owe you. I wouldn't have made All-Conference if you and Mick hadn't plowed holes for me to run through." Carl laughed. "And I wouldn't have gotten my mug in the papers with Gwen, the Homecoming Queen. Boy, was she hot."

"Yeah, too bad Mick got to her first and married her. Hey, cough up that phone number, and I'll get back to you. But meanwhile, see if you can pull some strings and get the coroner's report on Jeff."

"Got it. I'll call 'em today."

Pistol Pete Dalton's phone number was the NAVCAD barracks at Barin Field, but the cadet who picked up the phone said Pete wasn't around. I left a message with my home and work number and asked Pete to call me collect. I made sure it sounded official.

I also called *The Pensacola News*, but Jamie Lynn Jones wasn't in, so I left a message for her. Then, I reread the newspaper article. Carl was right—Miss Jones wrote well, but it still didn't make sense. Jeff landed in a farmer's field, plane undamaged, Jeff died. No, Miss Jones wasn't telling all she knew.

CHAPTER 2
The Shock

At the Sand Hills Police Department the following day, Connie walked into the office a minute behind me and asked if I'd called Carl and what he'd said. I told her what I'd learned and mentioned that I might get a call from Cadet Dalton and maybe a call from Miss Jamie Lynn Jones.

She sat in her roller chair behind the receptionist's desk and gave me the dreaded Connie squinted eye. "Miss Jamie Lynn Jones, huh? And who is she?"

"Oh, just another female reporter after my love and affection."

"Another, huh? So, who are the others?"

"You remember that reporter from Charlotte that covered the Christmas Tree Corpse murder last year?"

"The one with the beehive hairdo welded to her head with hairspray?"

"That's the one. Kept calling me for weeks."

"So, you prefer women with a wrestler's body and hairy legs?"

I glanced over my shoulder to the chief's office. Door closed; not in. I put my hand on Connie's shoulder and leaned into her ear. "No, actually, I prefer shaved legs and a trim but shapely body. Like yours."

"Dan!" Connie flushed, but she smiled when she said, "Go to your room, you naughty boy."

I went to my office and found a file on my desk that contained Officer Bullock's report on a massive new supply of moonshine on the streets of Sand Hills. I sat at my desk and read his observations and conclusion. It didn't fit; the local yokels wouldn't be so flagrant with the supply, so maybe this latest influx was part of something larger. Bullock had been on the late shift the night before, so I figured I'd wait until he came in at ten to discuss it with him. I'd just put the file on the corner of my desk when the phone rang.

"Line one for you, Dan. Collect."

"Thanks, Connie. Don't tell the chief." I punched the clear plastic button with the flashing red glow behind it. "Detective Lewis."

"Yes, sir, this is Cadet Dalton. You called, sir?"

"Yes, Pete Dalton, right? 'Pistol Pete.'"

"Yes, sir." The voice now had a smile to it.

"Okay, Cadet Dalton, thanks for returning my call.

I'm a good friend of Carl and Jeff Puckett, and I'm helping Carl deal with Jeff's accidental death. I understand you were on the same flight with Jeff when he went down. Do you have a minute to help us fill in a few blanks about the accident?"

"Yes, sir, but because of the accident, we've all got to be at a safety brief in twenty minutes, but I'll do my best to help for the next fifteen minutes."

"The briefing room is that close?"

"Oh, yes, sir—just down the street."

"Okay, here goes: Where did Jeff's airplane go down? How far away from Barin Field?"

"Not far at all, sir. I've heard it was maybe a mile or two southeast of the field."

"And he was with the flight the whole time up to the last few minutes?"

"Yes, sir."

"And what were the weather conditions around Barin Field when you returned?"

"There was a broken scud layer, or low, thin clouds with gaps, in the area at maybe four hundred feet above the ground. I had the lead, but I didn't have any trouble leading us back, and we made the break in the clear; that's where we fly over the field at five hundred feet and peel off one at a time to get in line to land."

"But the area around Barin was cloudy?"

"Low, thin clouds, yes, sir, but it wasn't a solid layer, so when we got to Barin, a clear break in the clouds above the duty runway allowed us to sneak in."

"But Jeff wasn't with you for the break."

"No, sir, I guess not. On the way back from the Gulf, as the lead, I focused on keeping a steady heading, altitude, and airspeed to keep it smooth for the guys on my wing. Then, a clean break and a good landing. So, I didn't know we'd lost Jeff until we landed."

"Could he have gotten lost in the low scud and separated from the flight?"

"No, sir. He would have been in parade formation with the rest of us, not in the scud."

"Where was the instructor when you made your break, and what is his name?"

"Lieutenant Hornsby. He followed us with the tow banner, so he might have seen something."

"Did you hear anything unusual during the flight home?"

"No, sir."

"But your canopies were slid back for landing. I've seen that in the movies."

"Yes, sir. We slide the canopy back on the downwind leg. And that fresh air is most welcome. The cockpit is only cooled by vented outside air, so it's like a sauna under that clear, bubble canopy when closed."

"So, with the canopy back, could you have heard

something like an engine backfire or sputter from Jeff's airplane if there had been anything like that?"

"I doubt it, sir. We have helmets with noise suppression ear cups, and there's the wind noise with the canopy back, and that R-eighteen-twenty engine in front of us is loud as hell, so…"

"Okay, I got the picture. Well, was Jeff okay? Health-wise, I mean? Was he a hundred percent, or was he dealing with a cold or something that might have caused him to lose consciousness or be woozy?"

"He was out late the night before and probably had a few beers. In fact, I think his girl had to sneak him back through the gate in the trunk of her car, but even though our brief was at six and he couldn't have gotten much sleep, he looked and acted healthy and alert to me—still the smart aleck wise guy."

"Wise guy, huh? Okay, his girl, that would be Betsy, right?"

"No, sir, this was Teri, Teri the Tiger Cub, Jeff called her."

"Young?"

"Seventeen, I think. The admiral's daughter. Lives mainside in Pensacola."

"Dating the admiral's daughter? That sounds dangerous to me."

"Oh, yeah," Pete said with a chuckle. "But that was

Jeff for you—nothing was too dangerous for him, especially girls."

"I see. So, was there a Betsy in his life?"

"Oh, yes, sir. Betsy McTavish or 'Bonnie Betsy,' he called her. Her folks are Scottish. Jeff met her at a dance at the USO club in Foley when I was dating her. They're really good to us in Foley; nice club, nice people. But after Betsy met Jeff, it was all over for me."

"So, she's from Foley?"

"Yes, sir. Works at Manning Jewelry on Laurel. I've got to go, Detective Lewis."

"Oh, sure, Pete. But one more quick question: Was Jeff a good pilot?"

"Jeff was a natural, sir. Smooth. Confident. If you're thinking he might have screwed up, forget it. Jeff was a 'Liberty Risk,' as we say, which means it was risky to let him off the base because he'd usually get into trouble. But once he strapped on that T-twenty-eight, he was all business."

"Thanks, Pete. Please let me know if you think of anything that can help us determine how this accident happened. Call me collect here or at home anytime."

"Yes, sir. Actually, I might learn something from the squadron safety officer at this briefing, but I've really got to go now, sir. Lieutenant Hornsby is a short-tempered screamer and hates anyone being late. I'll call."

My phone rang again around ten, and a soft, sweet woman said, "Detective Lewis? *The* Detective Lewis?"

"Yes, young lady," I said with a smile. "This is *The* Detective Lewis, super sleuth and defender of the people."

"Oh, horse pucky."

"What's up, Connie?"

"Line one again, but this time, it's a young woman who sounds southern to a fault."

"Ah, yes. Hopefully, that would be Miss Jones. I got it." I punched the flashing red glow again. "Detective Lewis."

"Jamie Lynn Jones here, Detective. You asked me to call you." Her voice did indeed have a sultry southern tone to it, but sultry with a no-nonsense edge.

"Yes, I did. Thank you for responding, Miss Jones. Or is it Mrs.?"

"It's 'J.J.' to my friends, Detective, but for now, I'm Miss Jones to you."

"Great. Thank you, Miss Jones. I called because I'm helping my old college friend and teammate, Carl Puckett, look into his brother's accident in the T-twenty-eight last Friday. I've read your story of the accident—very well written, by the way—and I'd like to learn more. In my experience, reporters are often asked to withhold information by the authorities, so I hoped enough time had passed that you were free to discuss it with me now."

"My follow-up article will be in this evening's paper,

so it will include all the information I'm free to release at this time."

"I'm in North Carolina. Will it be in the Charlotte or Raleigh paper?"

"Where did you see the Friday article?"

"In the Charlotte Sunday paper."

"Hum. I don't know if Charlotte will pick up today's article, but your friend, Carl Puckett, will see it in *The Pensacola News* tonight so he can fill you in."

"Miss Jones…can you at least answer this for me: Was there any sign of foul play? We suspect there might have been."

"If you call a bullet hole in the fuselage a sign of foul play, then the answer is yes. Or no."

"Or no?"

"Well, they were shooting at a target with live ammunition, weren't they? So, a stray round could have done the damage and been accidental."

"How much damage did it do?"

"I suspect enough to kill Cadet Puckett."

"Geez, he was shot?"

"By a fifty caliber round marked with paint, which makes it pretty easy to identify who shot him."

"How's that?"

"Each cadet in the flight was shooting rounds marked with either black, blue, green, or red paint. That way, they would know who hit the target and who didn't. And who scored bull's-eyes and who didn't."

"And what color was the round that hit Jeff's plane, and who was shooting that color?"

"I can't tell you."

"Is it in your today's article?"

"Nope. I'm still under a gag order on that subject."

"But you know."

"I spoke with one of the sailors over the weekend who armed the airplanes, so I think I know, but I haven't confirmed it."

"But the shot through the fuselage hit Cadet Puckett and killed him?" I said.

"Well, yes, and no."

"Okay, explain, please."

"Yes, it hit him and probably killed him, but I haven't seen the coroner's report, so I can't confirm that it killed him."

"Okay, is there anything else that wasn't in the Sunday paper that you can tell me now?"

"Again, Detective, I'm still under a gag order, so I can't tell you anything more than what's in tonight's paper. Get Mr. Puckett to read that to you."

"I will. I'll call him. Thank you, Miss Jones. I really appreciate your time. If you ever need background on the Puckett family, I'll be glad to help."

"Oh, well, thank you, Detective. I may just do that. Goodbye."

"Goodbye, Miss Jones."

"That's two collect calls this morning on the city's phone bill," Connie said as she stepped into my doorway. "How do I explain those and future collect calls to the chief?"

"Ah, come on, Connie. Does he ever check the phone bill?"

"No, but he does check the bottom line on the phone bill because it's the bottom line that subtracts from his budget."

"Okay, I'll donate an amount to the police department that will offset the collect calls. If you subtract that amount from the phone bill, the 'bottom line' will be unaltered." I grinned. "Come on. You're only pushing this 'cause you're jealous."

"Jealous of another hairy-legged reporter? I don't think so. Besides, my father taught me that jealousy was for insecure people and those with low self-esteem. I'm neither, so no, I'm not jealous."

"Well, good, because jealousy doesn't become you." I nodded at the cashmere cardigan she wore. "Now, that little yellow button-up cardigan does become you. Very nice."

"Thank you," Connie said as she touched the neckline

of the sweater. "A tall, redheaded detective gave this to me for Christmas."

"He must think you're someone special," I said as I walked toward her.

"I think he does, but…" She stepped up to me and put her arms around my neck. The front door opened. She dropped her arms. "Yikes, the chief."

I handed her the Bullock file on moonshiners.

"Take this to your desk," I said in a commanding voice, "and see that Officer Bullock gets it when he comes in. I want to see him right away."

"Sure, Dan."

The chief waited for her to pass, then stepped into my office, supported by his cane, his eyes squinted from the smoke rising from the cigarette in the corner of his mouth.

"Good morning, Chief," I said.

"Morning, Lewis." He cleared his throat. "I'd like to see you in my office."

"Sure. Should I bring a file with me? Is this about the moonshiners? Maybe the attempted bank robbery last week?"

The chief turned for the doorway and said over his shoulder, "Just bring yourself."

"Okay. Right behind you."

As I followed the chief out of my office, I looked

at Connie, who sat behind her desk and shrugged. I shrugged back.

The next few minutes in the chief's office were a shock. I'd never been fired before.

CHAPTER 3
The Crime

I wandered back to my office and felt Connie's eyes on me, but I didn't look up. I couldn't look up. Then, seated behind my desk, I put my elbows on the desktop and my head in my hands, trying to prioritize what I needed to do next. Dealing with Bullock and the moonshiners came out number one on the list. I wasn't leaving the Sand Hills Police Department without seeing justice done for Miss Jean Ann Tuley.

As evidenced by the report Bullock filed on the moonshiners in the area, he wasn't ready to take my place, but now he *had* to take my place. The hospital cases of methanol poisoning from bad moonshine were increasing, and Jean Ann had been among them. When Officer Bullock got to work, I called him into my office and asked him to explain why his report was incomplete.

"How do you mean incomplete?" Bullock said.

"You've identified a concentration of methanol poisoning cases at the Moore County Hospital in Pinehurst. Also, Saint's Hospital in Fayetteville, the dispensary at Fort Bragg, and scattered cases in between. What's the connection? We've never had such a diverse area of poisoning cases."

"Well, I don't know that there *is* a connection. Why would there be?"

"The pattern, Bullock, the pattern." I walked to the map on my office wall. "The cases take almost a straight line from Fayetteville and Bragg to Pinehurst with no cases north or south of that line. Why?"

"I don't know. Should I ask the doctors?"

"The doctors treat the cases. It's not their job to stop the cases from happening. That's your job!"

"Easy, Dan, you don't have to get all ticked off about this. I just heard you've been canned, and I hate it for you, but don't take it out on me."

"Bullock, when I'm gone, you're it. You're the guy that's going to have to keep the people safe around here, and that goes beyond traffic and parking tickets. I'm ticked off about this because people like Miss Jean Ann Tuley are going blind from methanol poisoning, and you're not taking it seriously."

"Well, Miss Tuley shouldn't have drunk that stuff. If she's stupid enough to drink rotgut shine, she deserves the consequences. Who is Jean Ann Tuley anyhow, and what is she to you?"

"Miss Tuley was Gunner Lum's fiancée. A sweet little nineteen-year-old. You remember Officer Lum?"

"Sure, yeah. Korean guy, right? Murdered last Christmas, right after I got here."

"Correct. Jean Ann took his murder hard, so hard she started drinking. That led to her losing her job at the Fayetteville Sports Club, and that led to her drinking the cheapest stuff she could find—moonshine. Connie and I tried to help her, but before we knew it, she was hospitalized last week with methanol poisoning and blind."

"Blind?"

"Yes, blind. That's just one disaster a batch of bad moonshine can cause."

"Yeah, but…"

"And why, Officer Bullock, was it so toxic this time? That wasn't in your report, but it should have been. Our local yokels know how to make good stuff, so why is the stuff out there now so toxic?"

"Heck, I don't know. Maybe they cut some corners. Maybe they got in a hurry and didn't sterilize the vats."

"And what are they using for the mash? If we at least knew that, we could focus on the farmers in the area who are growing that grain. I didn't see anything in your report that suggested you had the samples analyzed or even had samples. Do you? Have you?"

"Well, sure, sure I have."

"And sent them to Raleigh for analysis? Careful. I can check on this."

"Well, no. Didn't need to. I could tell it was corn liquor, probably from last summer."

"I want it analyzed, and I want it analyzed now. Get your sample to Raleigh in today's mail. And again, I can check on this."

"Okay, today's mail. No problem."

"And one more thing: Why is the supply so large? Is someone flooding the market for a reason, and if so, I want to know that reason. Do you know the reason?"

"Ah…well, no, I don't know. Forgot to ask."

"Then ask! Ask some of our guests, the guys we lock up to sleep it off. Get out there and dig, man. Get some answers. Got it?"

"Okay, okay, I got it, but, ah, what will happen to Miss Tuley?"

"She's in a home, a rehab home where they're trying to dry her out and teach her how to live as a blind person. Lum's insurance, some department money, and a little help from her family have gotten her on the way to recovery. Connie and I visited her on Saturday. She's making progress."

I walked back to my desk and took a deep breath. "Now, Bullock, listen to me. This will not happen again to anyone. Do you understand? We owe that to Jean Ann."

"Yeah, Dan, I understand. We'll stop it. We'll find 'em and shut 'em down." He gestured with his hand. "Ah… can I go now?"

"Please."

I spent the rest of the morning on the phone to the hospital in Fayetteville and the dispensary at Fort Bragg to see if they had any leads to the source. No one did.

Around eleven-forty-five, my phone rang, and a familiar voice said, "Lunch?"

"You bet," I said.

A few minutes later, Connie and I sat next to each other on stools at the end of the drugstore lunch counter on Broad Street. We ate our tuna sandwiches quietly, and then she turned to me and put her hand on my arm. I cracked a weak smile.

"Well, at least you have 'til the end of the month," Connie said, "and then another month's salary for severance pay. That's not bad."

"No, it's not bad at all. Could have been worse."

"And it's a budget thing? That's it? No other explanation?"

"That's pretty much it. The mayor told him this morning that the police department needed to tighten its belt, so I'm the weight he's chosen to lose. Then he thanked me for clearing up all those backlogged cases, complimented me on my work, diligence, etc., and said he'd give me a good reference letter, which you will no doubt get a chance to type."

"Well, it better be the best reference letter ever written. If it isn't, I'll see to it that it is before he signs it."

Connie paused, then added, "But that's not it, Dan. We could have found other ways to reduce department spending—not accepting collect calls, for instance."

I elbowed her, and she chuckled.

"Seriously," Connie said, "my guess is he's afraid the mayor will fire him before his retirement next year, and you will be the next chief, so he wants to remove that option. The mayor will have to keep him if you're gone."

"Yeah, could be. I think he's been living in fear of that ever since I got here. But it's done, so let's talk about my next move."

"That's what I'm worried about—that next move. There's nothing in all these little golfing towns around here for an experienced detective. For the last year, Pinehurst and the others have depended on you." She squeezed my arm. "I don't want to lose you, Dan."

"You won't lose me. I'm thinking I'll probably end up in Raleigh. That's not close, but it's not that far. I'll call a few contacts there and see what they say. And, hey, if worse comes to worse, I could return to the Army. Fort Bragg is close. I could even keep living here in beautiful downtown Sand Hills."

"Beautiful downtown Sand Hills, huh?" She hugged my arm and scoffed. "Like this was Beverly Hills or the Seven Hills of Rome."

"Well, it's beautiful when I'm with you."

"Ah, shucks, Detective Lewis, you are too smooth, you know that? I'm in love with a smooth-talkin' detective. Heaven help me."

"Unfortunately, you're in love with an out-of-work detective, so Heaven help us both. Or Heaven help us help ourselves, so I'll do that when we return to the office. I'll call Cal Timmons in Raleigh. He taught the Detective Licensing Course I took last year. Good guy. Knows everybody who's anybody in law enforcement."

"Good plan," she said, reaching for her iced tea.

Cal Timmons wasn't in. The receptionist at the Raleigh Law Center said he was on assignment in Washington and wouldn't be back until Thursday. I left Timmons a message and then asked to speak with Sergeant Arrowood, who I knew from a forensics class I'd taken. He was also out, so I left a message for him. My next call was to Asa Winegarden, Chief of Police, Chapel Hill, North Carolina. I was put on hold for ten minutes, but he finally picked up.

"Winegarden."

"Asa, this is Dan Lewis in Sand Hills."

"Yeah, yeah, Dan, Dan Lewis. Good to hear from you, Dan. What's up?"

"I'm looking for a job, Asa. My chief here in Sand Hills has decided to trim the department, and I'm the trimee."

"Oh, man, I hate that. That's not smart of your chief. He's giving up that department's future and his town's security."

"I tried to explain some of that to him, but he's made his decision, so my question is, do you have any openings?"

"I wish I did, but I just added a guy last week. Now, he came from the University Campus Police, so they might be looking to fill his position. Not much pay, but good bird watching and very little drama."

"Who's the contact there, and do you mind if I use your name?"

"The chief there is Lou Kipp. Use my name and tell him to hire you, or I'll come over there and beat him over the head with the golf trophy I took away from him at last year's tournament."

"Okay, thanks, Asa."

"No problem. Hold on. I'll get Alice to give you Lou's phone number. Good luck, Dan, and keep in touch."

As soon as I hung up, my phone rang, and I picked up.

"Can you talk?" Connie said.

"Sure."

"Your hairy-legged reporter from Pensacola called while you were on the phone, so I took a message."

"She did? Not collect, I hope."

"No, not this time. She said there's no point in you calling Carl Puckett tonight because her follow-up article on the T-twenty-eight accident has been spiked. The Navy has closed ranks and isn't talking to the media."

"Hmm. Wonder what they're hiding? Maybe she shouldn't have told me about that bullet hole."

"Bullet hole?"

"Yeah, I'll tell you later."

"Well, she thinks they're hiding something, and she's determined to go over their heads to find out what it is."

"That should be interesting. Maybe she knows Drew Pearson, that syndicated columnist who writes 'The Washington Merry-Go-Round.'"

"Better than that. She knows Senator Walker Wiremann, Chairman of the Senate's Appropriations Committee. He's her uncle."

"Wow. Uncle Walker, huh? Well, that should open up the Navy. Anything else from our hairy-legged friend?"

"She's not *my* hairy-legged friend, but that's all she had to say." Connie paused, then said, "You know, Dan, my cousin is in the Navy. I don't know where he's based, but I remember he's in some part of the aviation branch. Should I see if I can find him?"

"Heck yeah. The odds aren't good that he's in Pensacola, but it won't hurt to find out. And even if he isn't in Pensacola, he might know someone who is. Maybe a former shipmate."

"Okay, I'll call Aunt Tilly and locate him."

"Great. Meanwhile, I've got one more call to make."

Lou Kipp, Chief of Security on the University of North Carolina campus, picked up after one ring. We talked for ten or fifteen minutes. I told him about my situation and Asa Winegarden's threat with the golf trophy, which brought a hearty belly laugh, and then he put me on hold. A minute later, I heard the phone go live again.

"Dan."

"Yeah."

"Okay, I've got something for you. We've been talking with a couple of young guys who want to train for the job, but no decision has been made yet. So, if you can come to Raleigh tomorrow, I'd like to show you around and talk with you about the position."

"That sounds great, Chief. I'll see my chief about it this afternoon and call you back. Will that work?"

"Sounds good, but get back to me before four—got a tee time with the school president. And Dan…"

"Yes."

"Call me Lou, okay?"

"Sure. Thanks, Lou."

I hung up just as Bullock entered my office with his uniform cap in his hand.

"Ah, Dan, got a minute?"

"What's up?"

"Well, I talked with Dodge Grumps. You remember; he was in here last week. Old guy. Foggy eyes, limp."

"I remember. So?"

"Well, Dodge said the stuff out there now is really sweet, even sweeter than last year's shine."

"And…"

"And he thinks the stuff is coming from Fayetteville."

"Okay, and…"

"And… yeah, so, that's it." He ran the rim of his cap around in his hands.

"That's it as far as it goes, Bullock, but why do the poisoning cases go from Fayetteville all the way to Pinehurst?"

"Ah, I forgot to ask, but I doubt Dodge would know that."

"Did you find out where he got the stuff? And when?"

"He wouldn't tell me."

"But you asked."

"Ah…sure, I asked, but he wouldn't tell me."

"Maybe I'd better talk with Dodge. Where is he?"

"He was in the park behind us feeding the squirrels. But he's probably gone by now."

"I'll check the park, but meanwhile, find somebody else. Slimey Mac was in here last week for a couple of days, so find him. And ask the right questions."

My phone rang. "Yes, Connie."

"Sergeant Arrowood from Raleigh is on the line for you."

"Thanks." I looked at Bullock. "Go. Get some answers." Then I punched the flashing red glow.

"'Rat,' is that you?" I said.

"Oh, heck, Dan, aren't you ever going to let me live that down."

"No, of course not. That was too funny, man. Still cracks me up. I'd never seen anyone go from standing on the ground to the top of a barrel in one leap."

"Hey, the damn thing took me by surprise."

"Well, in your defense, that was the biggest alley rat I've ever seen, as big as a small cat."

"Yeah, and where was a cat when I needed one? Anyhow, what can I do for you, Dan?"

"What's your staffing situation, Allen? My department is downsizing, and I need a job."

"Oh, sorry to hear that. You loved Sand Hills."

"I still do, but under the circumstances, I'll have to give it up."

"Well, your timing is good. We have a guy retiring after a thirty-year career in homicide. That's going down in…three months. That'd be perfect for you."

"Three months, huh?"

"Yeah, could you wait that long?"

"Gee, I don't know. But I'd like to come over there and look it over. Maybe talk with the guy that's retiring."

"Great idea. Cal, the boss Cal Timmons, will be back Thursday, and I could make sure Big Jim is here. Jim is the guy that's hangin' it up. Maybe we could all get together. Could you be here for lunch on Thursday?"

"I'll be there, Rat, err, Allen."

He laughed and said, "Looking forward to it, Red. See you Thursday."

I sighed with relief and leaned back in my swivel chair. I had options, neither of them the perfect option, but at least someone wanted me. Then the phone rang again.

"Yes, Connie."

"Carl Puckett called while you were on the phone. Wants you to call him back collect. They're an hour behind us, so no hurry. We chatted a bit. Nice guy."

"Did he tell you why he'd called?"

"No, but his voice was upbeat, so maybe he's got some good news."

"Good news would be they've finally told him what happened to Jeff. Or maybe he's got the coroner's report. Anyhow, thanks, Connie. I've got it." I punched the flashing red glow.

CHAPTER 4

The Eavesdroppers

Carl's secretary connected us immediately.

"Hey, Red, thanks for calling back."

"Sorry I couldn't take your call, Carl. What's up?"

"On the accident front, unfortunately, nothing. The Navy has sequestered the instructor and the other guys on the flight and sealed the records of the accident investigation team, so I don't know any more than I did yesterday. But I do have some encouraging news, so hopefully, you'll feel the same."

"What's that?"

"First, can you take a leave of absence or vacation or something and come down here for a couple of weeks?'

"That'd be kinda hard to do right now, but I could do it at the end of the month."

"Oh. Well, that might work, but sooner would be better."

"What's the urgency?" I said.

"Cadet Pete Dalton has been charged with Jeff's murder and is in the brig."

"What?"

"Yeah, and even worse, they've got a new guy, a rookie, in the Naval Judge Advocate General office, Navy Lieutenant William Flood, and assigned him as the counsel for the defense."

"Wait a minute. They think Pete killed Jeff? Good Lord, why would they think that?"

"That's just it; they haven't said what killed Jeff or why they suspect Pete. They won't even let me talk with him. They said Lieutenant Flood was Pete's defense counsel, and I should talk with him."

"Did you? Talk with Lieutenant Flood, I mean."

"I couldn't get him on the phone. And he wasn't in when I went by his office on base."

"Well, they must think Pete had a motive. Can you think of a motive?"

"Only that Pete was really in love with a girl named Betsy, and Jeff took her away from him. And then Jeff was mistreating her as usual; two-timing her, of course, which was Jeff's usual practice with girls."

"Okay, that's weak. It's a motive for some misguided people, but I don't think it applies to Pete. When I spoke with him this morning, he mentioned Betsy but didn't sound upset over losing her. Still, even with a motive, there must also be means and opportunity. Just how do they think Pete did it and when?"

"They won't say. That's why we need you down here. And soon, before this rookie attorney gets Pete convicted, and the real murderer gets away with killing my brother. Please, Red. I want justice for Jeff."

"Geez, Carl, I—"

"Look, here's the good news: I've spoken with my law partner, the head shark in the office, and he's agreed to hire you. Understand? The firm wants to hire you as a P.I. to investigate this mess. He's met Pete a few times and agrees that, motive or not, Pete would not kill Jeff or anyone else. Well, except for someone in a Russian MIG-seventeen who was trying to kill him. And he could do it, too. They don't call him 'Pistol Pete' for nothing."

"So, he was doing well in gunnery?"

"He's done well with any weapon they've put in his hands. He holds the record score at the N.A.S. Pensacola pistol range with the thirty-eight, and according to Jeff last week, he's got more bull's-eyes on the air-to-air gunnery target than any of the others in his flight. The guy's a deadeye."

"I wonder if that's played into their conclusion that he's the guilty party."

"Why would you say that?"

"Oh…well, I was just thinking out loud here. Trying to think the way the Navy is thinking."

"You think they think he was shot? Maybe after he landed? But Pete couldn't have done that; he was still landing his T-twenty-eight at Barin."

I was afraid I'd already said too much, so I tried to wrap it up before I said more.

"Yeah, you're right. If that's what they're thinking, they're way off base."

"Darn right. But they must not think Jeff died in the aircraft during the accident. Unless they believe Pete somehow tinkered with Jeff's aircraft, and it crash-landed. But the paper said the airplane was undamaged, which doesn't fit. See what I mean, Red? We need you down here, man. There are way too many blanks we need to fill in."

"Let's go back to the rookie defense counselor they have for him, this Lieutenant Flood."

"Yeah, Lieutenant William Flood, a graduate of some unaccredited law school in California who managed to pass the law exam and get a Navy commission. So now he's got the right to *practice* law on my brother's friend."

"But wouldn't Pete be able to hire a civilian lawyer?"

"He would, and he will as soon as I get to talk with him. My boss is the head defense counselor in the firm, and he will represent him—pro bono."

"That's good. That's very good."

"But we still need a bloodhound down here we can trust, Red. And hopefully, that's you."

"Let me talk with my chief. I have some vacation time coming, so he might let me go for a week or two. And if he agrees, I'll be there on the next train."

"Ah, that's great. That's a relief. Thanks, man. Call me, okay?"

"As soon as I have a yes or no, I'll call."

"And if it's a yes, you're immediately on the payroll, and I'll send you an advance via Western Union."

I hung up, leaned back in my chair, and tapped my fingers on the armrests. Then I buzzed Connie and asked her to join me in my office and close the door.

"I can tell by the wrinkles in your forehead that you've been doing some deep thinking," Connie said after taking the chair beside my desk. "What's going on?"

"Carl has offered me a job with his law firm as a private investigator, a salaried job. The catch is he needs me there now. One of Jeff's best friends, Pete Dalton, who was with him on his last gunnery training flight, has been arrested and is in the Navy's brig at Pensacola."

"If Pete Dalton has been arrested, then they must think this is a murder case and not just an aircraft accident case."

"Exactly. It could be both, of course, but the fact that they have Pete in the brig tells me the Navy believes murder came before accident."

"What are you going to do?"

"I have a week of vacation coming, so I'll apply for that today and leave tomorrow."

"The chief's not going to like that, not with moonshine patients in the hospital and an attempted bank robber on the loose."

"Well, what's he going to do? Fire me?"

"My guess is he won't approve your vacation request, so if you leave anyhow, he may fire you *and* cancel your severance pay."

"I could appeal that with the mayor."

"Yes, but you'd have to stay here to do it."

"Ah, rats, Connie. I've gotta help Carl. And it's a job and steady income, so I wouldn't miss any paychecks."

"But it's a time-limited job. What happens after you help Carl, help Pete, then the case is closed? Even if they want to keep you on, would you want to stay in Pensacola? Would you want to be a career P.I.?"

"I'd rather stay here with you and be a detective for Sand Hills, but right now, that may not be an option."

Connie sighed. "Let's take a break and see about those wrinkles." She stood, stepped around behind me, and massaged my temples.

I closed my eyes, let my mind relax, and let the answer come. Then I patted Connie's hand, pulled a legal pad from my desk, and wrote my vacation request. My next move would depend on the chief.

Connie took my request just as the phone rang at her desk.

"I'll be right back," she said and kissed my cheek. "Relax. Whatever happens, it'll be okay."

I had just reached for the phone again to call Raleigh when Connie buzzed me.

"Yes, Connie."

"Got some bad news. That was the Moore County Hospital on the phone. They've admitted a patient this morning with lead poisoning. He's in a coma."

"Moonshine?"

"That's what they're saying, and they aren't happy that nothing has been done about it."

"Have you told the chief?"

"Not yet."

"Tell him, and tell him I'm working on it. Oh, and hold the vacation letter for now."

"Okay."

Next, I called Connie's son, Nate Hawke, and caught him just as he'd come in from school. I could hear Superman barking in the background, so I waited while Nate went outside and let him out of his pen, also known as the "Superman Suite." That first-class chain-link dog pen even had an elevated dog house with a sundeck.

"Detective Lewis?"

"Yeah, Nate."

"I'm back. I'll exercise Superman after we talk. What's up? I hope Mom's okay."

"Oh, yeah, she's fine. I'm calling to ask a favor of my very best assistant detective."

"Really? Oh, that's great. What can I do?"

"Some undercover work. And fast. Are you still friends with Mable, the waitress at Benny's Diner downtown?"

"Yes, sir. We're good friends. She's on my paper route and always gives Charlie and me an extra squirt of cherry syrup when we order a cherry Coke at the diner."

"That sounds like a friend, alright, so here's what I want you to do: Ride down there on your bike this afternoon when business is slow and see if you can get her to chat with you for a few minutes."

"That won't be a problem. Usually, the problem is how to get away from her. She loves to chat."

"Okay, good. Now, you know we've been dealing with moonshiners off and on for years, right?"

"Yes, sir. Especially from old Looper Heister, the guy that shot the chief."

"Well, it's gotten out of control lately, and people are ending up in the hospital."

"Oh, yes, sir, Mom told me about Miss Tuley. I really like her."

"So do I, Nate, and so I've got to find out who is making the moonshine and where they're making it so we can shut them down and not have more people go blind like Miss Tuley. But I'm not sure it's Looper Heister this time. Or his boys. They are the most likely, but it could be someone new."

"Who do you suspect?"

"I don't have any suspects yet, but this is where you come in. Maybe I'll have a few after you talk with Mable and get her to tell you the latest moonshine gossip at the diner. Will you do that for me?"

"You want me on the case?"

"I sure do. Just like last year when you helped me solve Officer Lum's murder. People will talk with you, Nate, or at least not be bothered if you boys are within hearing distance of their conversations. They won't always talk with an official like me."

"Can Charlie go with me?"

"Of course. You guys are a team."

"Okay. I'll call Charlie."

"Do that, then come down here on your way to the diner, and I'll give you money for cherry Cokes and burgers. Agreed?"

"Yes, sir." Nate paused. "But Detective Lewis...does Mom know about this?"

"Not yet, but I'll talk with her before you get here."

"Okay. Good luck."

I buzzed Connie. When she answered, I said, "Do you need to see Helen this week?"

"Helen, as in Happy Helen's Hair Salon?"

"That's the one."

"I don't *need* to see her. Why? You don't like my hair? Too long?"

"No, I love your hair but need some undercover work. Where in town does one go to get the latest gossip in Sand Hills?"

"Oh, I get it. What kind of gossip are you looking for?"

"See if you can find out where this moonshine is coming from and, if possible, who is brewing it and who is buying it."

"You suspect Helen's husband? I thought he gave that up years ago."

"No, no, not Ralph. Not anyone in particular. I just want to know what the gossip around town is about moonshine. Crazy Clara is usually there in the afternoon, so get her talking. And, if she's there, try to keep her on topic and don't let her wander off into the astrology weeds."

"What if her chart today says she shouldn't share gossip?" Connie said with a snicker.

"Then I don't guess she'll be any help. Will you do that for me?"

"I guess so. What are you going to be doing?"

"I've got to find Dodge Grumps. He's the closest lead I have right now. Oh, and Nate and Charlie will be here in a few minutes. I've asked them to help as well."

"And just what did you ask my son to do, Detective?"

"Nothing without your permission, I assure you. I just want Nate and Charlie to go to Benny's Diner and keep their ears open. They might hear something, or Mable might have some information."

"So, you want to flood our little township with eavesdroppers? That's your plan, Detective Lewis?"

"That's the plan. Are you in, Detective Assistant Connie?"

"Oh, I don't know. I'm kinda busy here at my desk. You know, typing letters and all."

"Okay, okay. Dinner at any restaurant of your choice but within a ten-mile radius."

"Dan, that would be Benny's Diner! Come on, let's go to our place in Fayetteville, The Steak House. You haven't taken me there since Valentine's."

"Okay, The Steak House it is. Man, you drive a hard bargain."

"Ah, shucks."

I came across Dodge Grumps as he left the park and crossed our parking lot. Head down, crumpled fedora on the back of his head, and with his oversized and untied clodhoppers slapping the asphalt, he limped along and mumbled something about helping Rodney.

"Hey, Dodge," I said. "Hold up a minute. Who's Rodney?"

"Oh, hey, Detective Lewis. Who's Rodney, you say?"

"Yeah, who's Rodney, and what's his problem?"

"He's my favorite squirrel, and I don't know what's wrong with him. He just ran up the tree trunk, froze, did a back flip, and now he's lying belly up with his little legs in the air."

"Lying where?"

"In the pile of oak leaves at the base of his tree."

"Was he chased up the tree?"

"No, but he was chased a little while ago. That old fat lady on Georgia Street with the German Shepherd let her dog chase him, then after they moved on down the park, Rodney came down from his tree and over to me for a drink. The fountain isn't working again, so… you city folks need to fix that, you know? Well, so, poor Rodney needed a drink, so I gave him some of my water."

"Let me see your water, Dodge."

Dodge held up a clear quart bottle that was labeled "Gin."

"You gave him gin?"

"No, no, not gin. This is sweet water from Slap Jack."

"May I?" I held out my hand, and he gave me the bottle. I took a whiff. It wasn't water.

"Who is Slap Jack?" I said as I returned his bottle.

"Some guy. I need to help Rodney. I've got to go."

"Don't go yet. I'll get help and be right back."

"No, I've got to see about Rodney. Get help and meet me at the first park bench."

I met Dodge at the bench with a full cup of tap water, but Rodney wasn't there.

"He was right here." Dodge pointed at the pile of leaves. "Suppose a cat got him?"

"I think he recovered from the sweet water and is back up the tree. I'm sure you'll see him tomorrow, but meanwhile, describe this guy Slap Jack to me and tell me where you met him."

"Ah, I don't remember. Must have been last week. I just don't remember. And it was dark, so he was just a guy. Short guy, I guess. My size."

"That's it?"

"Yeah, I need to go now." He pulled his fedora down to his forehead. "Got to get home." He limped off toward the street.

When I returned to the office, Nate, Charlie, and Connie were waiting for me. Connie held the boys back and motioned for me to join her in my office.

Once inside, she shut the door and said, "Carl Puckett called. He's got a hot lead for you, a Navy ordnance guy who's been transferred. Carl said he needs you there *now* before the guy has to leave. He sounded desperate."

"Give the chief my letter, keep your fingers crossed that I don't have to jump ship, then I'll call Carl."

CHAPTER 5
The Road Trip to a Murder

Connie returned to my office five minutes later with tears in her eyes. I hugged her and eased her into the chair by my desk.

"Hey, hey, what's this all about?" I said.

She sniffled. "I gave the chief your letter; he read it, then he cussed at me! He's never done that before. I know his leg has been bothering him, and he eats aspirin all day to numb the pain, but there was no call to use all those cuss words at me."

"It was my fault. I should have delivered that letter myself."

"That would have been better, but we didn't know he would go whacko on us." She blew her nose into a hankie. "Anyhow, he tore up the letter and threw it at me like confetti."

"That sounds like a definite no to me." I hugged her

shoulders. "Okay, so that settles it. I'm sorry, Connie, but I'll have to leave on tomorrow's train. But like you said, 'It'll work out.'"

She stood and hugged me. "Oh, I know it will. You'll straighten out that mess in Pensacola, come home, the chief will apologize, and things will return to normal."

I nodded. "And I'll take you to The Steak House."

I called Nate and Charlie into the office and explained to them and Connie that they would solve the moon-shine case and nail the mysterious Slap Jack. I would guide them from Pensacola, but first, I wanted to know everything they could find out that day, and then we'd put the pieces together that night. The missing pieces of the puzzle would tell them what to do next.

The next day, as the train rolled away from Sand Hills toward South Carolina, and with money in my pocket from Carl's firm, I read on my legal pad all the moon-shiner clues my eavesdroppers had come up with and discussed the night before. Mable at the diner had heard Looper Heister's boys talking about "Slap Jack" and his Cajun accent, and they didn't sound happy about the competition. The ladies in Happy Helen's said they'd heard the source was in Fayetteville, and Slap Jack was young and always showed up in city parks on Friday nights. Crazy Clara, the astrologer, said because it was Mercury retrograde, anything she said might be mis-understood, so she wouldn't comment. The boys would continue to eavesdrop, and Connie would see that Bullock would continue to work the case.

I had told Bullock in no uncertain terms that his job was to get a good description of Slap Jack—height, weight, facial features, scars, tattoos, hair, everything—even his gait and clothes. I got him started with Dodge's description. I felt sure I knew where to look, and with more details, I could put my finger on that guy. But my instincts and the fact that the guy had flooded the market told me it had to be soon.

The day before, once I'd decided to leave, I'd called Lou Kipp at the University of North Carolina Security and told him I had to take a job in Pensacola for now. He wished me well and said I would always be welcome there if I changed my mind.

Then I called Sergeant Allen "Rat" Arrowood in Raleigh and canceled my Thursday lunch with him and Cal. He agreed to reschedule the lunch for when I returned from Pensacola and reminded me that I had a few months to consider the vacant homicide position.

I leaned back, listened to the clackity-clack of the wheels on the track, swayed back and forth in my seat, and fell asleep.

I arrived at the L&N Passenger Depot in Pensacola at 4:25 the following morning. Carl met me in his three-piece lawyer suit and tie and loaded my suitcase into his black '55 Chrysler. Then, we drove three or four blocks to the San Carlos Hotel on Palafox Street. On the way to the San Carlos, Carl slapped me on my shoulder, thanked me for coming, and talked about the Navy ordnance sailor who would meet us for breakfast at the hotel. I checked in, showered, and met Carl at seven in the hotel restaurant.

While we sipped coffee and waited for the sailor, Carl asked about my job with the Sand Hills Police and when I needed to be back. I said, "No hurry."

"Oh, that's good, but won't that nice lady I spoke with yesterday miss you?"

"You mean Connie, our receptionist?"

"I got the impression she was more than that, Lover Boy."

"Ah, now wait a minute, Carl. Sure, she's special; in fact, she's wonderful, but there's no tuxedo in my future."

"You sure? I'd be happy to get mine out, dust it off, and stand for you."

"Look, I think your marriage to Caroline was meant to be, and I'm happy for you, but it's not my time. Besides, Connie is a Korean War widow with two teenage children, and one of them, Becky, the oldest, hates my guts. That's a domestic train wreck I don't need in my life right now, so no—no wedding bells for me."

"I'm not buyin' it, but I'll let it go for now." He checked his watch.

"It's been thirty minutes," I said. "Why don't you call that sailor and get him over here?"

"I don't have his number. I've never had it. He's called me a couple of times, but each time he was more secretive than the last."

"Did he give his name and rank?"

"Just his name. Sam."

"Well, what did secretive Sam have to say?"

"He said he had some information about the accident, Jeff's accident."

"But he wouldn't say what that was?"

"He said he was in aviation ordnance and knew who was shooting what color rounds the day of the accident. When I asked what that had to do with the accident, he said he didn't have time to explain, but he'd meet me and explain then."

"So, you suggested the San Carlos?"

"He suggested it. Said he was leaving Pensacola and would meet me here this morning before he left."

"For breakfast?"

"Yeah, but maybe he doesn't eat breakfast as early as we do."

We were ready to give up and ask for the check when a man in a gray fedora and tan trench coat walked up to the entrance to the restaurant. When the guy turned his back, I poked Carl on the arm and nodded at the guy.

"Carl," I said, "who's the Sam Spade wannabe in the entrance? Could that be your sailor?"

"I don't know."

Carl stood and walked toward the guy. I waited. After the two met beside a marble column at the entrance to the restaurant, they shook hands and looked over at me. Carl said something, and then the trench coat guy nodded and held out his hand. Carl pulled out his wallet and gave the guy a bill. The guy gestured for more. Carl gave him another bill. The guy gestured for more, but Carl snatched the first two bills out of his hand, pushed him away, and turned for our table.

The guy grabbed Carl's arm, and that's when I stood and pushed my chair back with a loud scrape on the wood floor.

Carl stopped. The guy let go and brushed Carl's arm like he was apologizing. Carl gestured to him like he wanted information. The guy talked for a minute. Carl returned the two bills to him, and the guy left.

Carl returned to our table and said, "I don't know about you, Red, but I could use another cup of coffee."

"Sounds good to me, but what the heck was that all about?"

"That was Sam, the sailor who needed a little spending money for his trip to San Diego, although I doubt Sam is his real name."

"San Diego being his next duty station, I presume."

"Correct. He said all four sailors on the armament team on the day of the accident had been transferred and ordered not to discuss the accident. And they'd been transferred in four directions—one to sea duty."

"That would explain the disguise, although I noticed the Navy trousers and shoes under that trench coat. There were Shore Patrol sailors at the depot, so he must have to travel in uniform, but he didn't want to be seen in uniform talking with us."

"Exactly. I guess he'll pack up the fedora and trench coat before he gets to the station."

"What else did he say?"

"Said Cadet Dalton was shooting red rounds, and a red round killed Jeff."

"How does he know the round killed Jeff? Has he seen the coroner's report?"

"No, but he said he'd heard from a buddy in the dispensary where they took the body that a red round hit Jeff, and there was a lot of blood in the cockpit."

"Could you tell Jeff had been hit by a red round when you saw the body?"

"They only showed me his face."

"Oh, okay. Well, if Jeff was hit by a red round, that explains some of the murder charge, but did he say how that was possible? How Pete could have hit Jeff?"

"Didn't say. Just said Dalton was shooting red, a red round hit Jeff, and he saw Jeff's plane go down."

"He saw Jeff's plane go down? He saw that?"

"He watched it. He said the flight approached the field in a sloppy parade formation, but everything looked routine until they made their break over the field. Then, as number four, Jeff came around for the downwind leg, he suddenly leveled out, descended, disappeared into the scud to the east, popped out under the scud but in an erratic turn, and then disappeared behind some pine trees. Then, the crash crew at Barin took off toward Highway Ninety-Eight and turned east. Five minutes later, Sam heard more sirens go by the field heading east."

"I'm wondering how Jeff could have been hit over the Gulf and still fly back in formation as far as he got. Maybe the wound wasn't that bad, but he had lost so much blood he fainted or was losing consciousness and couldn't keep the plane in the air any longer."

"That makes sense." Carl let the waitress top off his coffee. "But if he was hit during the shooting, why didn't he tell somebody, you know, make a 'may-day' call?"

"Good question. Maybe his radio was also hit. But back to Sam's story. If the sirens, probably an ambulance and a fire truck, were going to the crash scene southeast of the field, they must have come from...where? What's west of Barin?"

"Foley, Alabama. Small town."

"Okay, we go to Foley. And Barin Field is on the way?"

"Yeah, it'll be on your left off Highway Ninety-Eight just before you get to Foley."

"Good. We can check out Barin on our way."

"I can't go with you. I'd like to, but I'm due in court at nine o'clock."

"So," I said with a grin, "that explains the three-piece gray suit and bold red tie."

"Ah, yeah." He glanced at his tie. "It's an important corporate case, and Caroline says I've got to look more powerful if I'm going to win this case and improve my chances in the election."

"Election? You're getting into politics?"

"State House of Representatives. Her father is retiring."

"And Dad wants to keep it in the family, huh?"

"Something like that. Look, let's go to my office. I'll set you up with an expense account, and then you can take a cab."

"Okay. How far is it to Barin?"

"An hour's drive."

When we got to Carl's office, just two blocks away on Garden Street, the receptionist, a gray-haired, well-dressed woman in black accessorized with gold jewelry, smiled and handed me two messages.

The first message read, "Please call," and had a phone number and the name "Jamie Lynn Jones." The second read, "Hairy Legs called. She'll be in touch. Be careful."

I smiled at the second note, then at the receptionist, who smiled back. No messages remained secret on her watch.

"Thank you," I said.

Carl nudged me. "Problem?"

"Ah, no, no problem. That reporter wants me to call her."

"Jamie Lynn Jones?"

"Yeah. Have you talked with her lately, and if so, did she have any new information?"

"She said the paper spiked her follow-up piece on the accident, but that's it. No news."

"I don't know why she's called me, but I guess I'll find out." I motioned to Carl for us to move away from the prying eyes and ears of the receptionist.

At a tall palm, I stopped and said, "Instead of a cab, how about a rental car? Wouldn't that be easier on the expense account?"

"Yeah, I guess so. National is here now, but they're so new I didn't think of that."

"Okay, I'll look them up, get a car, and call Miss Jones. I should be in Foley by eleven. I'll be at their hospital if you need to get in touch. Foley does have a hospital, right?"

"Gee, I don't know. Maybe. Or at least a doctor's office."

Carl left for his court appointment. I called Miss Jones from my room, but she wasn't in. I left a message.

I called National and asked for a basic Ford sedan, but when I got to their lot on Garden Street, they only had a new 1956 Ford Fairlane Sunliner Convertible, Golden Glow Yellow, with a V-8 and an automatic transmission. I said that wouldn't do. They said I could have it for the basic Ford price. I drove away in the convertible with a map by my side.

Fifty minutes after leaving National, driving west on Highway 98, I passed Barin Field Road on my left but decided to press on to Foley and see what I could learn in town first.

I stopped at what looked like the only traffic light in Foley and noticed a sign on the second floor of a two-story building on the southwest corner that read, 'Holmes Hospital, Dr. James Holmes, M.D." Below, on the first floor, was Crosby Drugs. With a green light, I crossed McKenzie Street, or Highway 59, parked on the right side, then crossed the street to the hospital and entered on the first floor.

The lady in a stiff white uniform behind the wooden desk had a dignified air, short gray hair, and a pleasant smile. I introduced myself as a friend of the deceased NAVCAD pilot, Cadet Puckett, and his family. In a British accent, she introduced herself as Alina but didn't want to discuss the accident. She did acknowledge that

Dr. Holmes had been at the accident scene and offered me a chair if I wanted to wait to speak with the doctor, who was upstairs treating a patient.

"Alina," I said, "was there anyone else from your hospital at the accident scene, maybe a nurse?"

"I recall Dr. Holmes went alone. He had to leave a patient with Miss Anderson, the nurse."

"Did the doctor say anything about Cadet Puckett's condition when he returned?"

"I couldn't say, Mister Lewis. You need to speak with the doctor but remember, sir, there is doctor-patient confidentiality, you see, so I don't think you'll get much information from him. I suggest you contact the Navy."

"Unfortunately, Alina, the Navy has refused to discuss the accident with family, friends, or the media. And speaking of the media, has a reporter from *The Pensacola News* been to see the doctor?"

"Yes, a Miss Jones stopped by yesterday—a very chatty, attractive young thing, you know." Alina clasped her hands and placed them on top of a logbook on the desktop. "She didn't get answers either."

"Alina." A man's voice came from the top of the narrow wooden stairs along the far wall.

"Yes, doctor?"

"Do you remember that pharmaceutical rep that came by last Friday with the new asthma drug delivery device, the aerosol device?"

"Yes, doctor. He left only one sample, but it's here in the sample cabinet."

"Bring it up, please."

"Right away, doctor." Alina stood, removed a small, white box from the white cabinet against the wall, crossed the room, and then took the stairs.

I jumped up, flipped the medical logbook on the desktop back to Friday, and read, "Treated Cadet Puckett for shock, a GSW, and facial lacerations. CPR protocol administered, but couldn't keep a pulse. Patient expired."

I heard footsteps on the stairs, closed the logbook, and sat. So, sailor Sam was right; I knew "GSW" stood for gunshot wound. But from where? And when?

CHAPTER 6
The Giggling Nurse

As Alina left the stairs and crossed the room, I could tell by the way she avoided eye contact that I wasn't going to see the doctor that day, but I expected it and had a backup plan; there had been others on the scene besides the doctor.

"I told Doctor Holmes you were here," Alina said as she resumed her position behind the desk, "but he apologized and said he couldn't see you or discuss the accident. I'm sorry."

I stood. "Oh, that's disappointing, but thank you for asking. I appreciate it. Uh, before I drive back to Pensacola, where does a guy go to eat lunch around here?"

"The Foley Coffee Shop is up the street on North McKenzie and serves light lunches, but if you want barbeque, there's Billy's on South McKenzie, or you can get fried chicken at Dottie's Chicken House on West Orange Avenue. That's a block south."

"Where do the police and firefighters eat," I said with a smile.

"Oh, they are coffee junkies, you see, so they eat at the Coffee Shop where they get unlimited refills."

"Thanks," I said and turned for the exit, but stopped and looked back. "Alina, did the fire department respond to the accident?"

"Yes, indeed. They were right behind the doctor."

I thanked Alina again, then walked to the Foley Coffee Shop two blocks up North McKenzie. From lunches with my fire department friends in Sand Hills, I knew that if firemen had anything in common, they loved talking about their experiences. So if a bullet killed Jeff, and they were willing to talk about it, I had a good chance of learning where it entered the cockpit, the size of the hole, and why the Navy was so sure it was a red bullet that killed him.

The Foley Fire Department turned out to be directly behind the Foley Coffee Shop, so I wasn't surprised to see two tall men in blue firefighter uniforms enter from the back as I entered from the front. They took the first booth on their left, and I took the booth in front of them with my back to the one with fair skin and freckles.

The conversation behind me started when the fair-skinned guy said, "Your turn, right?"

"No, no, you sorry skate artist," the suntanned one with the close-set eyebrows said, "it's your turn." Paper rustled. "See? Right here. I wrote it down this time. Monday, I bought lunch for Skate."

"Oh, that must have been last Monday. I bought yesterday. Remember? You had to have the second piece of apple pie?"

"*You* had the extra pie, you lyin' hose monkey, and I paid for it. Yesterday."

"Fellas, fellas," I said as I stood and faced them, "excuse me, but would you both do me a favor and let me buy your lunch today? My name is Dan, and my dad was a firefighter, and I'd like to do this in his memory. How 'bout it? And hey…double apple pie all around."

"Sounds good to me," the fair-skinned guy said.

"Sure, mister," the tanned one said, "and you're welcome to join us. I'm Chad, and this lyin' piece of you-know-what is Eric, commonly known as Eric the skate artist or Eric the lyin' Viking." He slid over toward the wall, and I sat.

"You're Norwegian?" I said as I faced Eric.

"No, but my grandparents were."

A tiny gray-haired colored waitress in a checkered apron stepped up to the booth. "Okay, boys, if you're through arguin', what's your order?" She pulled a pencil from her curly hairdo. "As if I couldn't guess."

"The usual, Miss Lilly," said Eric, the Norwegian descendent.

"Same," said Chad, "but extra lettuce, tomato, onion, and pickles on mine, please."

"Dat double cheeseburger is too tall for your small mouth already, Mister Chad. How you gonna eat it with all dat extra stuff piled on it? You want a knife?"

"A steak knife, please."

Miss Lilly shook her head, then looked at me. "For you, suh?"

"A BLT, please. With fries."

"And sweet tea all around?"

We nodded.

"Got it," Miss Lilly said as she stuck the pencil back in her hair. "Now, boys, before you ask. We don't got any apple pie today. We gots peach, and dat's it." She turned and walked toward the counter with her head high.

"She's a pistol," I said.

"She sure is," Chad said. "She's been here forever, so ask Miss Lilly if you want to know anything about Foley."

"Well, on that subject, I'm a private pilot, and I'm really interested in what happened here in Foley last Friday, so maybe she can help me. I understand a T-twenty-eight trainer crashed near here. You guys know anything about that?"

They looked at each other, and then Chad said, "We

weren't there, but the guys that were there have been told not to talk about it."

"Did the guys that were there, your fellow firefighters, I presume, ever say anything to you guys about it? I mean, don't worry—I'm not with the press, but the papers said the plane crashed. Was there a crash?"

They looked at each other again, and then Eric said, "It just landed in the field is all we know. Didn't crash. Just landed. But our guys didn't get close enough to tell us more than that. The Barin Crash Crew guys did all the work. Our Foley Fire guys were just there in case the crash or landing caused a fire."

"Yeah," Chad said, "the Barin guys would know more than our guys."

"Suppose they'd talk with me if I went to the base?"

"Ha, I doubt it," they both said in unison.

"I'm sure you're right," I said and smiled.

The lunch finished with vanilla ice cream on peach pie with coffee and the two firefighters telling me about the 1922 fire that burned down the town. They said Eric's father was in on that one and had the ember burn scars on his shoulders to prove it. I left a two-dollar tip, and then we walked to the fire department so they could show me around.

Around two-thirty, I returned to the Foley Coffee Shop, where Miss Lilly cleaned up after the last customer.

"I figured you'd come back," Miss Lilly said as I walked in the back door.

"Why's that, Miss Lilly?"

"Nobody leaves a two-dollar tip 'less by accident or dey wants somethin'." She straightened the salt and pepper basket and ketchup on the table. "What you want?"

"I want to know if you know any of the Barin Field Crash Crew guys?"

"Yessuh," she said as she straightened. "I knows all of 'em. Dey eat here on Sunday when da mess hall is closed."

"Have you heard them talk about the T-twenty-eight accident last Friday?"

"Yessuh."

"I'm sorry I didn't introduce myself before, Miss Lilly, but my name is Dan Lewis, and I'm very interested in that accident. It's personal." I motioned toward the nearest booth. "Here, if you don't mind, please step into my office and tell me about it."

"Your office, huh," she said with a chuckle.

"Yes, ma'am. From now on, when I'm in Foley, this booth will be my office."

"Humph," Miss Lilly said as she looked over her shoulder.

I looked. No one there.

"Okay, Mr. Dan. Two minutes. I gots to get back to my house before my grands gets home from school. I keep 'em for my son and his wife so dey can work." She sat.

"What have you heard," I said as I slid onto the booth seat across from her.

"Well, Mr. Dan, dey weren't supposed to talk about it to anyone, but I heard dem talk amongst dem selves, and dey said dey pulled dat Cadet Puckett out of da cockpit, laid him out—da boy was soaked in blood from his ribs on down—and tried to keep him breathin', but dey couldn't."

"Did they say anything about the condition of the plane?"

"Said it was okay. Said Cadet Puckett did a good job of landing it, but I don't see how. But dat's what dey said."

"And why was there so much blood?"

"He done been shot, dat's why. Big bullet hole in da left side of da airplane right next to where da boy be sittin'. And da strange part is there was red paint around the bullet hole like it done scraped off da bullet."

"Did they explain that?"

"Said it must have been from one of da other pilots on dat flight."

"Where was it? The landing, I mean. Who's field?"

"It be Mr. McTavish's field. And hey, I done forgot dat part. Dey also said he done come runnin' up to da plane just as da crash boys got there. But he took a quick look, den he took off."

"McTavish? Like he was afraid?"

"Like he was scared dey done blame him."

"Why would he think that?"

"Well, I don't know. And da crash boys didn't know or didn't say, but I know Mister McTavish is one of those *Mountain Men*. Dat's what dey call dem selves. Dey shoot black powder. Maybe dey was a shootin' dat day."

She stood. "I really gots to go, Mr. Dan."

"Got any donuts left?" I said as I slid out of the booth and stood with her.

"Yessuh. Ten cents."

"Just put one on a napkin for me, and I'll get out of your way." I handed her a dollar. "And keep the change." I winked. "I'm on an expense account."

On my walk back to my rental car, a tall, curvy young blonde in a nurse's uniform approached me on the sidewalk.

"Mister Lewis," she said as she smiled and stopped before me. "Or should I say, Mister *Detective* Dan Lewis?"

"Uh oh, someone's blown my cover," I said and smiled back.

"Yeah, we caught cha, but don't worry; your secret is safe with us." She motioned me to join her on a wrought-iron bench on the sidewalk before the Hotel Magnolia. It faced a park on the other side of the street.

I took a handkerchief from my back pocket and brushed the street dust off the bench for her.

"Oh, my, Monsieur Detective Lewis, how gallant," she said as she sat.

"Please call me Dan," I said as I sat beside her. "Now, Miss…"

"Anderson, Amy Anderson, but you may call me Amy."

"Okay, Amy, now what do I owe the pleasure of your company?"

"I work with Dr. Holmes. I'm on a late lunch break now, but Alina got a phone call for you and wanted me to deliver the message. She thought you'd be at the Coffee Shop." Amy gave me another one of her perky smiles.

"Okay, what's the message?"

"Oh, sure." She cleared her throat. "Miss Jamie Lynn Jones wants to meet you at Captain Ahab's restaurant on Palafox this afternoon. Five o'clock."

"Black tie?"

"No, of course not." She chuckled. "Sounds like a business meeting for cocktails to me."

"You know this restaurant?"

"Oh, yes. Very upscale. Jeff—that is, Cadet Puckett—took me there a couple of times."

"Oh, so you knew Jeff?"

"Oh, yes, we dated, but Jeff dated all the girls. He was fun and liked to spend money, but about as faithful and dependable as the weather, plus he expected a little too much in return for a meal, if you know what I mean.

So, it didn't bother me when he threw me over for Betsy McTavish."

"Are you dating someone now?"

"Oh, my, Dan, are you asking?" She glanced at my empty ring finger. "I'm flattered."

"No, I, ah…"

"It's okay," she said with a giggle. "The answer is yes. I'm seeing Cadet Rhoades, 'Dusty,' a strong guy from Portland, Oregon." She made a muscle. "A lumberjack kind of guy."

"Was your lumberjack, Dusty, in the same flight as Jeff when Jeff had the accident? If so, have you talked with Dusty about it?"

"Dusty was the number two guy, the first guy on Pete's wing."

"Sounds like you speak the lingo," I said as I leaned back.

"Hey, you date a few of these guys—and I have over the past year—and you learn to speak their language and recite their procedures. I could fly that T-twenty-eight myself just from listening to them brag about it."

"What did Dusty tell you about that day and that flight?"

"I only talked with him the afternoon they got back, then the C.O. confined them to quarters and wouldn't let them talk. But Dusty didn't know what happened. He just said the whole flight was screwed up, like someone had put a hex on it. It was their last gunnery flight, and they expected to do well: To fly a tight formation out there, get good hits, and fly back for a Blue Angel kind of breakup and landing."

"Did Jeff do okay out at the target?"

"Dusty didn't say. Just said the whole mission was sloppy. I'm sorry, Dan, but he didn't like Jeff. None of them did. I think Pete was the only one who tolerated him."

"Why didn't Dusty like him? Was it because you had dated him?"

"Oh, no, not that. I think Jeff owed Dusty some money. Jeff was always borrowing money. As I said, he liked to spend money on girls or at the dog track, even money that wasn't his. Took me exactly one and a half dates to figure that out."

I stroked my chin. "Amy, help me with this question: If Pete had accidentally, or on purpose, shot Jeff during the gunnery mission, how could that have happened?"

She sat back on the bench, held her hands out in front of her with her fingers together, and then shot me a sly grin.

"Okay, Dan, this is how they talk. See? With their hands as airplanes."

"Okay."

"So, let's say my left hand is Pete, the flight leader, and my right hand is Jeff, number four in the flight, or "dash four" as they say." She spread her hands out. "And a thousand feet below us and ahead of us is the instructor, Lieutenant Hornsby, who nobody liked either. He's flying the tow plane with the target a thousand feet behind him."

"Where are numbers two and three?"

"They're over here with Pete, joined up on my left hand. They've already made their pass and climbed back up to join Pete on the left side of the target. That only leaves Jeff, dash four, to make his diving pass from the right side and then join the rest of them on the left for the next pass." She dove her right hand down past her knees, then turned it up toward her left hand.

"But let's say," she said, "just as Jeff finishes his pass and pulls up, Pete rolls in early for his next pass at the target and squeezes off a round." She twisted her left hand to the right and swooped it downward. "The round hits Jeff's airplane as he's climbing up."

"Is that what happened?"

"Who knows?" she said with a shrug. "It would explain how sloppy Jeff's flying was on the way back, but the guys don't know what happened. Dusty said he thought Pete rolled in early but didn't say Pete fired early."

Amy stood, and I stood with her.

"I'm sorry, but I've got to go," she said. "Lots of patients this afternoon, so I just have time to grab a sandwich for Alina and me and take it back."

She gave me a hug, as southern girls do, and suggested

I be careful with Miss Jones. I didn't get a chance to ask why before she was off to the Coffee Shop.

On my way out of Foley and on the drive back to the San Carlos in my yellow convertible, I noticed a street sign two miles past the Barin Field sign that read, "McTavish Road." So, now I knew how to find the accident scene, but I had an hour's drive ahead and just enough time to clean up and change for my command performance with Miss Jamie Lynn Jones, or "J.J." to her friends. I smirked. And Amy had warned me about her. Maybe Miss Jones had also dated the late, swashbuckling Jeff Puckett and was more Jeff's speed. I preferred to think she had finally seen the coroner's report and was ready to share it with me.

CHAPTER 7
The Surly Reporter

When I returned to the San Carlos and asked for my room key, the desk clerk peered over his reading glasses and held his finger to his lips like the location of my key was a secret. His nametag read, "Emmett." Behind him, I heard voices from a side office, including one irate female voice. I nodded and waited.

A door opened behind the clerk, and a large woman in a small, squashed red hat with black netting burst into the space behind the counter. She slapped her hand on her hat and shot over her shoulder, "And your hotel will never host another of my events again! Ever!"

The woman hooked her black purse over her arm, brushed past the clerk, and stormed around the end of the counter and through the lobby.

"Whew," I said. "What zoo did she escape from?"

"The Navy Zoo," Emmett said as he twisted his head

left and right to be sure he wasn't overheard. "That's 'Hat-pin Harriet,' the admiral's wife."

"Oh, I see. Difficult, huh?"

"Mm-hmm," he said as he retrieved my key and handed it to me along with a note. He picked up the phone, and I saluted him goodbye.

I was halfway up the staircase when I glanced at the note and stopped. I looked down and located the phone booths along the wall outside the restaurant, then descended the stairs. Emmett supplied me with enough quarters for the long-distance call. As usual, the phone booth smelled like an ashtray and had burn marks on the phonebook ledge, but the folding door closed tight, the overhead light came on, and the call went through.

"Hawke residence. Nate speaking."

"Hey, Nate, Dan Lewis here. Is your mom available? I have a note to call her."

"Mom just got home, and then she and Becky went shopping for a dress. Prom night is coming up, and some poor sucker has asked Becky to go with him."

"Well, the note said she had some information pertaining to the Slap Jack case. Do you know what that's about?"

"Oh, yes, sir. That's the scoop Charlie and I came up with. We saw the guy. Well, we didn't realize we'd seen the guy, but after Charlie and I went over the clues after school today, we realized we really did see the guy. Last Friday night."

"Where and what did he look like?"

"At the park, or in the parking area along the edge of the park. He jogged out of the park wearing dark clothes, boots, and a knit cap. He ran through the light of a streetlamp, then he jumped into an old black car and took off. A Dodge sedan, I think."

"Okay, but what makes you think that was our guy?"

"He had an empty canvas bag in his hand, and his car had Louisiana plates. Didn't somebody say he had a Cajun accent?"

"Yeah, they did. It's in my notes. Big guy, or small? Thin or heavy? And which direction did he go?"

"Maybe five feet five or six, medium build, drove off toward Pinehurst."

"And his clothes? Well dressed? Jeans, overalls, or what?"

"Looked to me like he did his shopping at the Army-Navy Store. Definitely not well dressed, but not country, either. Oh, and overdressed for a warm evening."

"Got it, Nate. Good job. Give your mom a hug for me and tell her I'll call the office in the morning. Okay?"

"Yes, sir. Oh, one more thing. His car had a dented rear fender that rattled when he drove off. Left rear."

"Oh, man, you're good, Nate. Two burgers on me next time. Goodbye."

A five-block walk down Palafox toward Pensacola Bay brought me to Captain Ahab's restaurant with its Spanish-style facade and a wrought-iron balcony on the second floor. Through the large floor-to-ceiling windows on the ground floor, I could see ceiling fans, palms, and fish nets cluttered with dried shellfish hanging from the walls. A crowd filled the stools before a long bar across the back of the smoke-filled room.

A rosy-cheeked brunette in white shorts and a white U.S. Navy jumper uniform top with the black neckerchief met me inside and handed me a bar menu. When I told her I was there to meet a Miss Jamie Lynn Jones, she smiled and motioned for me to follow her to a table-for-two against the front wall to my left.

"Be careful," she whispered as we walked to the table. "You're late."

"Geez, only ten minutes," I whispered back.

"'If you're not early, you're late,' sayeth Miss J.J."

Miss J.J. wasn't at the table. I sat. The cute sailor with a nametag that read, "Tina," left two bar menus on the table, smiled, and patted my shoulder as she departed. Ten minutes later, a young woman with long brown hair and pale blue eyes approached the table. I stood.

In a brown business suit that did a poor job of hiding her curves, she plopped her leather purse on the table and stood by her chair.

"I'm Dan Lewis," I said. "You must be Miss Jones." I pulled her chair back for her.

"You're late, Detective Lewis," she said as she sat.

"My apologies, but so are you." I returned to my chair.

"I was here at four fifty-five, Lewis. You weren't here at five."

"So, you got your feelings hurt and left? A little tit-for-tat?"

"What?"

"Look, Miss Jones, I've had a long night and a long day. I can help you, and you can help me, so let's get to it and stop playing childish games. Why did you invite me here?"

"Why you...just who do you think you are to talk to me like that?"

"Just another citizen who wants justice for Jeff Puckett. And who do you think you are? You're acting like a spoiled brat cotillion queen." I smiled. "And you look like one too. Nice hair with just enough wave, and you wear your makeup well. But the suit and tie? No, don't like the suit."

"Well, who asked you to like the suit?"

"You wore it in public, so you must want people to like it."

"Get my chair," she said as she grabbed her purse off the table.

"I take requests, but I don't take orders," I said as I stood, "so if you're ready to go, then go."

She pushed her chair back and stomped off.

I sat and picked up the bar menu. I'd just gotten to the beer list when a hand touched my shoulder.

"I thought that went well, didn't you?" Tina said.

"Oh, sure," I said, looking up at her. "If you like fire-fights."

"A firefight that you handled well. I'm glad somebody had the guts to put that woman in her place."

"Not your favorite customer?"

"Not hardly, Mister…"

"Dan Lewis, from North Carolina. Please call me Dan."

"Gladly. What can I get for you to ease your post-fire-fight tension, Dan?"

"A Bud and some peanuts, please. If you've got 'em."

"Got popcorn."

"Popcorn it is."

"And don't worry," Tina said as she leaned over to me. "J.J. went to Trader Jon's across the street. She'll cool off and come back."

"Thanks for the warning."

Tina patted my shoulder again and walked toward the bar.

I had finished two beers and a bag of popcorn and moved to the other side of the table to watch the entrance when Miss J.J. reappeared through the restaurant door with her suit coat unbuttoned and a rolled-up newspaper under her arm. She saw me and pointed a manicured fingernail at me. Judging by the sloppy grin on her face, she had finished her share of toddy-for-the-body over at Trader Jon's place and had not cushioned its effect with popcorn.

Tina greeted her and took her arm, but J.J. snatched it away and staggered toward me. Tina followed with a furrowed brow and arms ready to absorb a J.J. crash.

"There you are, you rude man," J.J. said as she stopped and leaned on my table. "Are you ready to apologize to me and talk business?"

"Hello again, Miss Jones. I'm ready to talk business, but I've already apologized to you."

"You have?" she said as she straightened.

"Sure. You remember?" I stood. "Let me get your chair."

"Oh. Okay. Thank you."

I pulled her chair out for her, and she sat. I made a cross-eyed funny face at Tina and returned to my seat. Tina chuckled under her breath, then made an eating motion, and I nodded.

"Let's get something to eat, Miss Jones," I said. "What would you like?"

"Oh, eat? We need to talk business."

"Yes, we do, but first, how would you feel about some crab cakes?"

"Crab cakes. Oh, yes, crab cakes. My favorite. With coleslaw. They have delicious coleslaw here. Very sweet. I love sweet coleslaw."

Tina returned with the food menus, so I ordered crab cakes, slaw, rolls, and butter. And coffee.

After a hot roll slathered with butter and the first crab cake, Miss Jones stopped slurring her words but also lost the grin.

"Did you see the evening paper?" she said. "It just hit the street."

"No, I didn't."

"Here. Page one." She handed the rolled newspaper to me.

I put my fork down and opened the paper to read the headline, "Robert 'Scotty' McTavish arrested and charged with manslaughter." The byline read, "by Jamie Lynn Jones."

"Well done, Miss Jones," I said. "Tell me about it."

"The Navy finally spoke to me this afternoon just in time for me to get this to press. It seems Scotty—and I know that old goat well—was behind his house test-firing a Civil War musket he wanted to buy, and he wanted to make sure it was accurate. He had another musket he *knew* was accurate, so he'd marked the tips of the Minié balls they fired with paint: Red paint on the balls in the new musket and yellow on the balls in the old musket. He used a plywood target a hundred yards across the field behind his house."

She took a bite of the second crab cake and chased it with coffee. I followed suit.

"Okay," she said. "So, just as Scotty is sighting in on the target, his wife opens the back door, and Scotty's coon dog, Scratch, runs out of the house and jumps up on Scotty's legs. Scotty buckles, pulls the trigger, and the shot goes up through the scud layer of clouds and hits Puckett's airplane just as it came around after the break. And unfortunately, also hit Puckett."

"And that shot had red paint."

"Correct, and because it was a fifty caliber Minié ball, it made a hole in the airplane the same size as the fifty caliber rounds the students use in the gunnery training."

"And left red paint around the hole."

"Correct."

"Did it also leave black powder residue around the hole? It would have if that's what happened."

"Oh, I don't know. They didn't say."

"I wonder if they even bothered to check. I'm sure the Navy would much rather this be a civilian-caused accident than a Navy training accident."

"I'm sure you're right, but the good news is Cadet Dalton was to be released this afternoon, and he and the others involved will be back on their training schedule tomorrow." She finished the second crab cake and dug into the coleslaw.

"Ah, Miss Jones…"

"Ah, heck, Dan." She swallowed. "Call me J.J."

"Oh, okay, J.J., have you seen the coroner's report?"

"No."

"Have you talked with Cadet Dalton's attorney, Lieutenant Flood?"

"No, I haven't. Why?"

"I just have a feeling this isn't over yet," I said. "I want to see that coroner's report."

"Even with Cadet Dalton cleared, they still might keep it from us, but I'll see what I can do. If they resist, I know a sailor who might do me a favor."

"Is that the same ordnance sailor who told you about the bullet hole in Jeff's plane?"

"That's the guy," she said. "Name's Sam. Or that's what he called himself. Very secretive."

"Sam is history," I said with a grin. "He's halfway to San Diego by now and probably living large on your money and Carl's."

"That rat!" She banged her fork on the plate. "I gave him fifty bucks because he told me he'd be around if I had more questions."

"Well, he won't be around because they transferred him and the other ordnance guys that loaded the planes on that flight. But maybe Lieutenant Flood can get it for us."

"Well, maybe. Flood hasn't been any help so far. In fact, it may be time to call my uncle Walker. He'll shake 'em up."

"As in Senator Walker Wiremann?"

"That's him. His votes in Congress have sent a lot of money to Pensacola Naval Air Station, so they owe him."

"Then let's get Uncle Walker in on this. Meanwhile, I'll see if Carl and I can make an appointment with Flood tomorrow."

"You know, Dan..." She swallowed another bite of coleslaw. "There's a Change of Command reception for the guy relieving Captain what's-his-name. I can never remember that guy's name, but he was the C.O. of the USS *Saipan*, the carrier they use for student carrier qualifications. Anyhow, it's tomorrow night at the Mustin Beach Officer's Club mainside."

She dabbed her mouth with the cotton napkin. "Would you like to be my escort? I'm willing to bet Lieutenant Flood will be there."

"Well, sure, J.J. ol' buddy. Tell me where and when to pick you up, and I'll be there."

"Six o'clock, The Palafox Place Apartments number three, just up the street."

That night, even though it was after nine o'clock in

North Carolina, I called Connie at her home. She picked up, and I could tell she'd been asleep.

"Sorry, Connie," I said. "But I wanted to hear your voice."

"Oh, well, thanks, Dan, that's sweet. I sure wanted to hear your voice and without Miss J.J. Hairy Legs in the background. I assume you've had your talk with her by now."

"We met this afternoon."

"Well?"

"Well, what?"

"Is she built like a wrestler, and does she have hairy legs?"

"She's actually quite attractive, at least until she opens her mouth. Very abrasive."

"You don't like abrasive."

"No, I don't. I like sweet, gentle, loving. Like you."

"Oh, my, there you go again with the smooth talk, you cad, but you must have been attracted to her."

"No, I wasn't. Now, remember, Connie, you're a self-confident and non-jealous mature woman. We just talked about the case, and the good news is Pete Dalton was released this afternoon. They've charged another guy, a farmer. I'll call the office tomorrow and fill you in."

"Collect? Better not. The chief is still prowling around like a wounded bear."

"No, darlin', not collect. By the way, have you heard from your Aunt Tilly about your cousin the sailor?"

"She promised to call me tomorrow but said Rick has been transferred to somewhere in Florida, so he might be in Pensacola."

"Okay. Hope so. Oh, based on my talk with Nate this afternoon, I think I know where you'll find Slap Jack. I'll also tell you about that in the morning."

"Looking forward to it, but Dan…if Dalton was released, can you come home now?"

"Not yet. That farmer they arrested may or may not be the killer, accidental or otherwise. There are still too many unexplained pieces of the puzzle to say it's over. Jeff's erratic flying, for example. I need to sleep on it and let you get back to sleep. I'll call you tomorrow at the office. Nite nite."

"Nite nite, you rascal."

CHAPTER 8
The Good Girls and Bad Boys

I met Carl at the San Carlos restaurant for breakfast early the next morning, but first, I stopped at the row of phone booths. Five quarters later, the phone rang at precisely 8:05 Eastern time at Connie's desk. She didn't answer. I watched people wander past me for another five minutes, then dialed again. No answer. I called her house. No answer. I looked up Officer Bullock's phone number in my pocket notebook and called him.

"Glenn Bullock," he said with sleep in his voice.

"Bullock, Dan Lewis, why aren't you at work? Why isn't *anyone* at work?"

"Worked late again. We need another guy, Dan. The chief is wearing me out, and you're not here to help. Where are you anyhow?"

"I'm in Pensacola, Florida, but what does it matter? I don't work there anymore."

"Oh, yeah. Sorry about that. I wish you were back, even if you'd still want to jump down my throat over little stuff."

"Little stuff? You mean like people going blind?" I sighed. "Listen, Bullock, no one is answering the phone at the office. That's not good. I want you to get there as fast as you can and find out what's going on. Will you do that for me?"

"Sure, Dan. Just let me get some coffee."

"Skip the coffee, man. Get to the office. I'll buy you ten cups of coffee when I get back. I'm going to call the office again in ten minutes. Will you be there?"

"Yeah, yeah, I'll be there. Ten minutes, that's...eight twenty-eight."

"Correct. Eight twenty-eight your time."

Carl knocked on the phone booth door and gestured toward the restaurant, so I hung up but gestured to him to wait a minute. I called the office again. No answer. I left the phone booth and walked with Carl into the restaurant.

"What's going on," Carl said as we were shown to a table by a window.

"I don't know. Connie's not at work or home. No one is answering the phone at work."

"It could be nothing. Maybe a traffic jam."

"In Sands Hills, North Carolina? There hasn't been a traffic jam in Sand Hills since the last Christmas parade when Jimmy Bobo's decorated self-propelled corn picker broke down, and the whole parade had to be diverted down a side street. No, I'm thinking it's something medical."

"I hope that's not it, but look…I saw the paper last night. You think that's what happened? You think Scotty accidentally shot at that airplane and hit Jeff?"

"I don't know. I wouldn't rule out 'accidentally on purpose' just yet. Wasn't his daughter, Betsy, dating Jeff? You told me that, right?"

"Yeah, I did."

"I'm going back to Foley today to ask more questions. Betsy works at a jewelry store there, so maybe she'll talk with me."

"What did you learn yesterday?"

"Only that Jeff had borrowed money from one of his buddies—Dusty—and hadn't paid it back. You know Dusty?"

"Never met him, just heard Jeff mention him."

"And Jeff had been playing the dogs again." I checked my watch. "I've got to call the office. Be right back."

Back in the phone booth, and much to my surprise, Bullock actually answered the phone.

"It's Lewis," I said. "What's going on?"

"The office was empty, the door was unlocked, but the chief's patrol car is here."

"Is Connie's car there?"

"No."

"Okay, call Doctor Emmerson first, then if Connie and the chief haven't arrived, call the hospital and see if they're there, and then call me back. Got it?"

"But you're long distance."

"I know that, Bullock. Just do it, and I'll tell the hotel to accept the charges." I gave him the hotel number, then walked to the front desk to tell Emmett about the call and asked him to page me when the call came through.

"I ordered for you," Carl said as I returned to the table.

"That's fine. I still can't find out what's going on with Connie."

"I'm sure it's nothing." He sipped his coffee. "Say, Red, the partners in my firm have been invited to a reception at the Mustin Beach Officer's Club tonight for the new skipper of the *Saipan*, and Caroline has insisted we go. Gotta press the flesh, you know. Care to join us?"

"You're not going to believe this, but after I met Miss Jones for dinner yesterday, she invited me to take her to the reception."

"You met her for dinner?" He leaned toward me. "Tell me more."

"Well, that's it. We just met for dinner and swapped information."

"And that's all you swapped?" he said with a nasty grin.

"That's all. Period."

"Okay, so did you learn anything more than what was in her article last night?"

"Only that the Navy did not say they had tested the hole in the airplane for black powder."

"Why—" Carl leaned back so the waitress could deliver his pancakes with butter and syrup. "Why would they test for black powder?"

"If McTavish shot Jeff either accidentally or on purpose, there would be black powder residue around the bullet hole in the airplane along with the red paint. If they didn't test for that, we still don't know who shot him. It still could have been Pete, which would explain Jeff's erratic flying back from the Gulf. My guess is that if the Navy had thought of it, they would have tested for black powder so they could blame McTavish and get the blemish off their training record."

"I think the operative word there is 'if.' Maybe they haven't thought of it."

"Well, maybe. If I get a chance tonight, I'll ask." I cut into my eggs. "The thing is, we still don't know if a bullet actually killed Jeff. And on that subject, did you or your head shark ever get a copy of the coroner's report?"

"Ah, no, we didn't. Or I don't think we did. I've been so busy with this run-for-office stuff I haven't talked with Cliff."

"Cliff would be the shark?" I took a bite of eggs.

"Yeah. Cliff Collier."

"That's the key, Carl. If it was a bullet that killed Jeff, and the hole in the airplane had black power around it as well as red paint, then McTavish is the guilty party. No black powder, then Pete did it, which would explain why Jeff's flying was so erratic on the way back, but only if the round also hit his radio." I chewed on my eggs thoughtfully. *I've got to see that airplane.*

"So, was Pete more in love with Betsy than we know and thus Pete's motive?" Carl said.

"That's a question I hope to answer today," I said as I mopped up the egg yolk with a piece of toast. "I'm going back to Foley. Meanwhile, do you know who is representing McTavish?"

"Ah, maybe I should find out."

"Maybe you should. Whoever it is may have the coroner's report or can get it."

A bellboy stopped at our table and said I had a call on the house phone.

I swallowed the last of my eggs and excused myself.

"Dan Lewis," I said as I picked up the house phone by the booths.

"Dan. Bullock. Bad news."

"Connie?"

"Oh, no, no, Connie's fine, but the chief has had a heart attack and is in ICU."

"Prognosis?"

"What nosis?"

"Prognosis, Bullock. What does the doctor say about the chief's chances for recovery?"

"Oh, they didn't say. Or Connie didn't tell me."

"Where's Connie?"

"She's on her way back here. The chief's wife is with him now."

"Then Connie should be there any minute now, so let's talk about Slap Jack. Did you get the moonshine sample results?"

"Today's mail. They promised me it would be here today."

"They didn't tell you what the results were?"

"Oh, yeah, they did."

"Well?"

"Sugar."

"The mash was sugar?" I said.

"Yeah, that's what they said over the phone."

"Did they mention lead?"

"Well, yeah, they did. Said there were traces of lead."

"Then we're after a female soldier from Louisiana stationed at Fort Bragg and working in the motor pool."

"What?"

"The number one crop in Louisiana is sugar cane. This female soldier is from a sugar cane area and probably learned her craft from her 'Granpappy.' She drives a Dodge with a dented left rear fender with Louisiana plates, dresses heavy to cover her shape, and has her hair in a knit cap to disguise her female hair. She also comes out at night because she works during the day on base and does her drops on Friday night because she doesn't have to make formation on Saturday morning. You got all of that?"

"Yeah, I guess so. So, what do I do now?"

"You go to Fort Bragg. At the base, you see Master Sergeant Hoffman at the Military Police Department. Tell him I sent you. I used to work with him. He's a straight arrow and a good law enforcement officer. Heck, he's probably been working on this case himself and will take your information with open arms."

"What if he doesn't?"

"You kick his butt, snatch the perp, and bring her to Sand Hills."

"Nah, you really don't want me to do that, do you, Dan?"

"Of course not. Chances are there won't be any problems. Remember and remind Hoffman: People are going blind, and people are being poisoned by lead because the perp is using old truck radiators to condense the mash liquid instead of a copper coil. And those radiators are discarded truck radiators from Fort Bragg's motor pool."

"Okay. Ah, hold on. I think I heard a car door slam out back."

I heard the back door squeak open, and Connie say, "Is that Dan?" Then footsteps.

"Dan?"

"Hi, Connie. How's the chief? And how are you?"

"I'm okay now, but it sure was a stressful morning. The chief is resting, but his heart is in bad shape. I don't know what they'll be able to do for him other than nitroglycerine to relax his heart arteries and then enforce bed rest."

"I'm glad he's still with us, and I'm glad you're okay. It worried me when you didn't answer the phone this morning."

"I'm okay."

"I've just been explaining to Bullock what he needs to do about Slap Jack. He knows where to go and who to arrest now. He can tell you about it, but he'll also need a letter from our—that is *your*—office to explain who he is and why he's there, so please help him with that. I've got to go, but I'll call you again tonight."

"Okay, Dan. I'll take care of it. Looking forward to your call."

"Me too, 'Bye."

On my way to Foley on Highway 98, a blue Ford with U.S. Navy stenciled on its sides exited McTavish Road and passed me going east toward Pensacola. I decided I'd start there and turned onto McTavish Road.

The McTavish home, a modest two-story frame house, sat between two live oaks and faced north from the end of a straight dirt and gravel road. A large barn with stalls for horses and rolling farm equipment sat thirty yards from the house and faced east. A Dodge pickup sat in front of the porch, and I could see the rear of another pickup parked behind the house. I parked beside the Dodge in front.

As I exited the convertible, a gray-haired woman wearing glasses and an apron opened the screened door to the porch.

"Hello," I said. "My name's Dan Lewis. May we talk?"

"Why should we?" the woman said from the half-opened door.

"If you're Mrs. McTavish, I may be able to help you."

"Aye, I'm Mrs. McTavish, but I don't need any help."

"I may be able to help your husband then."

"He doesn't need any help either. The crops are in for the spring."

"I may be able to help him *legally*," I said as I stopped at the steps to the porch. "I noticed the Navy has been here, and I've heard they have arrested your husband. I saw them leave."

"You're a lawyer then?"

"No, I'm an investigator. I find the truth in legal cases. I'm helping Mr. Carl Puckett figure out what happened to his brother Jeff that caused him to land in your field."

"Aye, his brother. Very sorry for him and the loss of his brother, but we've told the Navy everything we know, and they told me Scotty would be home soon, out on bail, you know. Now we want to be left alone."

"I understand, Mrs. McTavish, and I won't bother you, but I have just one quick question before I go. Did the Navy mention anything about traces of black powder discovered around the bullet hole in the airplane?"

"Nooo, no mention of that."

"Okay, thank you, Mrs. McTavish. Good day."

"Good day, lad." She slipped behind the screened door, and it squeaked closed.

In Foley, on Laurel Avenue, I passed the Holmes Hospital and parked in the next block in front of Manning Jewelry. Then I saw nurse Amy Anderson exit the hospital and walk my way toward Stacey's Drugs. I waved to her, jogged across Alston Street, and met her at the screened door to Stacey's.

"Hi, Dan," she said. "Come to flirt with me again, I hope."

"Now, Amy," I said as I opened the door for her, "you're taken, remember? And I don't want to tangle with a young lumberjack."

"You're funny," she said with a giggle. "Well, if you're not here to flirt with me, what brings you back to Foley?"

"If you have a minute, I'll tell you. And buy you a soda."

"Just let me give Miss Jackie this prescription, and then we can talk while she's filling it. But no soda. Got to watch my weight. Lumberjacks don't like overweight women, you know."

I took a table, and Amy returned seconds later, still smiling, and sat.

"Amy, how well do you know Betsy McTavish?"

"Well enough, I guess. We have lunch together sometimes. Good girl."

"What did she think of Jeff?"

"Oh, she loved Jeff. I mean really loved him." She pulled a napkin from the dispenser on the table. "You know, it's funny how girls go for the bad boys. Can you explain that, Mr. Detective?"

"I'm a detective, not a shrink, but as a detective, I've noticed some trends."

"Such as…"

"Excitement. Nice guys are predictable, and young girls like excitement, surprises, and even danger."

"Uh oh, you're hitting close to home now."

"And the girl always thinks that whatever the bad boy's problems are—drinking, anger, slovenliness—she can fix it. I've heard girls say, 'Sure, he has baggage; he drinks too much and has a short temper, but I can fix that.' They think 'true love' can fix anything. I call it the 'Beauty and the Beast syndrome.'"

"Can they? Fix it, I mean."

"Almost never. It's best to remember that you can't fix or change someone else. You can only change yourself."

"Humph."

"Did Betsy ever say Jeff had issues she could fix?" I said.

"No, but she did say she loved his spontaneity. But then she'd complain about him not keeping his promises. And, of course, she knew he was cheating on her."

"Was that with Teri, the admiral's daughter?"

"Among others, but Teri lately."

"And your guy? Does he need fixing?"

"Oh, he likes to play childish pranks, and he smokes and drinks like the rest. It's that fighter pilot image they see in the movies. I don't care for that, but nobody's perfect."

"And you can fix it when you're married," I said with a grin.

"Sure," she said, then chuckled. "Okay, you caught me."

"Do you suppose Betsy would talk with me if I went by the jewelry store?"

"Are you going to buy something? Something for your lady?"

"I hadn't thought of that, but a little sparkle from Foley might be a good idea. She deserves it."

"Then I'm sure Betsy'll talk with you."

"Okay, great. Could I buy you girls lunch? Say, Billy's Barbeque?"

"Sounds good to me. Unless we get a walk-in appointment."

"Okay, if Betsy agrees, I'll come by and check in with you. And tell Alina she's welcome to come along, or if she can't, we'll bring her a take-out."

Amy had to pick up the prescription and return to the hospital, so I waited for her on the sidewalk. As we walked to the hospital, I told her I had one more question.

"Shoot," she said.

"Pete was number one, Dusty number two, and Jeff number four. Who was the number three guy in that gunnery flight?"

"Oh, that was Jesse Durand, a colored guy and a good guy. Ohio State grad, but I think he's from Mississippi. He's gone to the dog track with us a few times." She waved and blew me a kiss. "Hope to see you for lunch, Danny Boy."

Amy returned to the hospital, and I turned around and walked up the street to Manning Jewelry. I didn't know if getting on the Barin Field base and talking with Cadet Durand or any of the others would be possible, but I'd give it a try. That would be after I entertained the ladies at lunch, and it's a good thing I did. Once they started talking, a piece of the puzzle I didn't see coming fell in my lap.

CHAPTER 9
The Graveyard Hangar

Manning Jewelry shared the south side of Laurel Avenue with the USO club that entertained the sailors from Barin Field with dances and parties. Having a jewelry store next to a hangout for sailors struck me as a marketing stroke of genius. Then staff it with the young, dark-haired beauty in the tight black sweater who stood behind the glass counter and greeted me, and that sealed the genius label.

"Welcome to Manning Jewelry," the young woman said as I entered.

Her large brown eyes held me captive for a second, but then I said, "Hi, my name's Dan Lewis and I'd like to see some bracelets."

"Of course, Mr. Lewis, my name's Betsy, and I'm glad to help. Just step over here."

"Betsy McTavish?" I said as I followed her around to a glass case.

"Yes. Do I know you?"

"We've never met, but I'm a friend of the Puckett family, and by the way, let me express my condolences for the loss of your friend, Jeff."

She paused beside the glass case and studied me with narrowed eyes.

"I really am here to see a bracelet, Miss McTavish. Honest. For my girl in North Carolina."

"And that's all you're here for?"

"Oh, I see." I smiled as pleasantly as I could. "I've met your mother, and your natural suspicion strongly resembles her guarded nature. And that's okay. I don't blame you."

"That's good because if you're here to discuss Jeff's accident, you're wasting your time. I don't know what happened, and I don't want to discuss Jeff. He's gone. He's old news."

"I got it. Now, I really would like to see a bracelet, a sterling silver bracelet. My girl, Connie, only wears silver."

She paused to study me again but then used the key she had with her to open the case.

"That one," I said as I pointed to a bracelet with an etching of vines and leaves. "It looks wide enough for an engraving on the back. Can you do that for me?"

"Sure, but it's extra."

"Of course. How much total?"

"Bracelet plus engraving, depending on how many words, would be fifty-two-fifty with four words. Say, 'To Connie. Love, Dan.'"

"Well, I don't know. I was thinking, 'To Connie, from Dan.'"

"You don't want to say 'love'? You don't love her?"

"Well, yes, I guess I do; I mean, she's everything, she's wonderful, but…"

"But you just can't say that word yet, right?" she said with a relaxed smile.

"I guess that's it. I don't just throw that word around, you know, so to put it in writing would be a commitment to me, and I'm not sure I'm ready for that."

"I understand, and I'm sure she'll appreciate it either way, but think about it, okay?"

"Okay," I said with a hesitant smile. "I'll think about it."

"But you still want to buy it today, right?"

"If I can make a down payment and put it on layaway until payday."

"I think we can do that, but I'll have to ask Mr. Manning, and he just stepped out."

"When will he be back?"

"At noon. That's my lunch break."

"Okay, and speaking of lunch, how would you like lunch with Amy Anderson and me at Billy's?"

"You're meeting Amy?"

"Yeah, we're friends. Come on and join us. I'm buyin'."

"That might be fun. I haven't seen Amy in days, and I need to discuss something with her." She held up her hand. "Discuss with *her*, Mr. Lewis. Girl stuff."

"Hey," I said with a chuckle. "I get it. I'll get lost when the time comes, but meanwhile, call me Dan, okay?"

"Okay, Dan. Come over to the counter so I can get your information and hold the bracelet for you until Mr. Manning returns." She took the bracelet from the case and relocked it. "I love this bracelet. Excellent choice."

Just after noon, Betsy and I left the store, picked up Amy, and walked a block south to West Orange Avenue, where the most delicious smell poured from a brick chimney on a brick building with a glass front. We waited outside a few minutes for a table inside, but it was worth it. The juicy meat melted in my mouth, and the sweet potato fries were large and crisp.

But I wasn't getting any juicy information from the girls until the table talk centered around who was dating who and who had dumped who. Pete's name came up when Betsy said she'd heard from him again.

"Oh, Betsy, that's great. I really like Pete," Amy said.

"Yeah, Pete's one of the good guys, but after my Jeff

experience, Daddy doesn't want me dating any more pilots."

"Betsy," Amy said, leaning over her plate, "Did your daddy really take a shot at Jeff's airplane?"

"He said he did—accidentally. He explained all that to the Navy. Scratch jumped him, and the gun went off. I'm sure he didn't intend to hit Jeff, but he told me he's glad he did."

"Betsy! He's glad?" Amy said.

"He didn't like Jeff one bit, Amy. Not since Jeff got me home an hour late on a weeknight with my clothes all messed up. That Jeff was all hands. You know that." Betsy glanced at me and back to Amy. "That's enough Jeff talk."

"Well, ladies," I said. "I think that's my cue to take care of the check. Be right back."

At the cash register, I looked back at the table where both girls leaned toward each other and seemed to be talking simultaneously.

We walked Amy back to the hospital, delivered a barbeque sandwich to Alina, and then Betsy and I continued to Manning. On the way, I said I was concerned about her father and how his attorney would handle the case.

"We're not worried. The attorney said the coroner's report would clear Daddy."

"That would be Cliff Collier? Your daddy's attorney? He's seen the report?"

"Ernest Applewait is Daddy's attorney. He's seen the

report, and apparently, there's something in there that proves Daddy may have shot Jeff, but he didn't kill him."

"That's great. What was it?"

"He didn't say. Just said Daddy would be cleared. Daddy's at home now, or he will be this afternoon. On bail."

"Oh, that's good. I'm happy for you and your family." I stroked my chin. "This new information didn't have anything to do with black powder, did it?"

"No, that wasn't mentioned, but Daddy was sure his shot hit the airplane, so I guess the hole in the airplane would have black power around it. Everything else he shoots with those muskets does." She stopped at the steps to the entrance to Manning.

"So, that wasn't it," I said. "That wasn't the information that will clear your daddy."

"Apparently not, but enough, Dan. I guess you're some kind of detective here to help the Puckett family, and that's okay; I like you. But I've said enough. Let's go see Mister Manning."

"Sure. No problem." I suddenly realized what some of that conversation across the table was about while I was paying the bill at Billy's. So much for my secret being safe with Amy."

With a downpayment made and my promise to reconsider the *love* word when the bracelet was paid in full and ready for engraving, I left Manning Jewelry, but not without a warning from Betsy.

"You can't just drive onto the base," Betsy said. "You'll need a reason for visiting and a pass, which requires a visit to the visitor's hut and some paperwork. The Marine at the gate will direct you."

Once in the visitor's hut, the best excuse I could come up with was that I was a friend of Cadet Pete Dalton, down from North Carolina, and I'd like to visit with him. The Marine behind the counter phoned Pete, and he acknowledged me, so I got my pass.

At Pete's barracks, a two-story wooden building with a veranda on each level and screens on the tall windows, I parked in the parking area in front and took the wooden stairs to the lobby.

Leather sofas and chairs, black ceiling fans, and a pool table completed the spartan look. Stairs led to the second floor on either side. Three cadets stood by the pool table.

I didn't have any problem recognizing one of the three as Pete. Of course, he had short hair, white trousers and shoes, and a stiff white shirt with epaulets that labeled all of them as cadets, but at six feet tall and athletic, he walked toward me with a relaxed swagger and confident smile that said he approved of himself. The nickname "Pistol" fit, and I could see him as a perfect match for Betsy.

The other two cadets paused to check me out while

Pete and I shook hands, and then we walked to the veranda to sit in the shade and enjoy a light breeze.

"Yours?" Pete said as he pointed to my yellow convertible.

"Oh, yeah. A rental and the last car they had, so I got a deal."

"Very nice. When I get my commission, I'm going to buy a Corvette—a red Corvette. I've already talked with the people at the Pensacola Buggy Works, so they'll order one for me."

"So, the commission is imminent?"

"All that's left is carrier landings, advanced instruments, and multi-engine training, so it's not imminent, but we're getting there."

"And no residual problems from the Puckett accident?"

"No, sir, I don't think so. I didn't shoot early, and none of the guys said I shot early, so the shot that killed Jeff didn't come from me. I think old man McTavish brought Jeff down."

"On purpose?"

"Wouldn't surprise me, but I don't know."

"Pete, where is that airplane now?"

"In the far left hangar," he said as he pointed down the street.

"Any chance we could see it?"

"We could try. The accident investigation team is

through with it, so it's probably just sitting there waiting to be cleaned up and returned to service. We better ask first."

"Who do we ask?"

"The Officer of the Day, probably."

"But he's just a regular pilot officer, right? Not a maintenance guy or someone in charge of the hangar."

"Probably."

"Then let's walk down there, and if we see someone in charge, let's ask them."

"And if we don't see someone in charge?"

"Then we mosey inside and take a look. If someone stops us inside, we say we didn't know who to ask for permission and apologize. In my experience in the Army, I found that getting forgiveness is always easier than getting permission."

"I don't know, Mr. Lewis. I don't want to do anything that will threaten my commission and my Corvette."

"I don't blame you," I said with a smile. "I'll just wander down there myself."

"No...better not. I'll go with you. But if we're stopped, you do all the talking, okay? I'm just a cadet taking orders."

"Deal."

At the end of the street, as we turned left to go down a line of four two-story brick hangars with curved roofs and open sliding doors that faced the hangar next to it, I noticed four pilots leave the first hangar and walk toward two rows of T-28s along the other side of the hangars. Beyond them, two T-28s taxied, and another roared down a runway.

"Do you know them?" I said as I pointed to the pilots.

"I've seen 'em around. I think they're in the fighter phase. That's the class behind us. They've probably just left the line shack in the hangar after checking the maintenance records on their T-twenty-eight. The guys lagging behind in the salty khaki flight suits and parachutes over their shoulders are the instructors. The one with the red helmet bag is Lieutenant Hornsby. He was our instructor, but they reassigned him as a fighter instructor when they grounded us after the accident."

"I've heard he's a hardass. Hornsby, I mean."

"He's not much loved, that's for sure, but he's a heck of a stick, one of the best I've ever flown with."

"Were you his favorite?"

"Ha, that's a joke. Hornsby doesn't have favorites. He's hard on everybody. Maybe harder on Jeff because Jeff was so casual about everything and often late to the briefing, but where Hornsby came from, he didn't get any slack, so he doesn't give any."

"Where was that? Where did he come from?"

"A farm in the sticks. Hard father. Hard work. Then, his brother got injured, and Hornsby had to work even harder. That's all I've heard."

"You've told me before that Jeff was good, but how are the other guys?"

"Rhoades and Durand are above average, I guess, so I'd trust either of them to cover my six. That was Rhoades at the pool table with me when you came in."

"The short guy with the broad shoulders?" I straightened. "That's Dusty?"

"Yes, sir. Why the surprise?"

"Oh, well, I know Amy Anderson. In fact, I had lunch with Amy and Betsy. Amy talks about Dusty all the time, but as she is so tall, I just figured...well, you know."

"Yes, sir, I know what you mean. They're kinda an odd couple, but it seems to work."

"And by the way, Betsy said she'd heard from you. Seemed pleased about it."

"Yeah? I'm not sure what to do about that. I'm surprised she seemed pleased."

"Her father has laid down the law about dating pilots," I said, "but it's got nothing to do with you."

"Oh."

"Just let it ride for a few days, let things settle, her father's arrest and all that. Things will work out."

"Will he be convicted and get jail time?"

"I doubt it. There's something else going on in the case that I hope to learn more about tonight at a reception at Mustin Beach. I'm counting on Lieutenant Flood, your former lawyer, to be there and answer some questions for me."

"Hey, I think Durand is going to be there. I hope you get to meet him. Good guy."

"Jesse Durand?"

"Yes, sir. He's a negro cadet and the only one in the program, so they like to show him off. Plus, he's a stud and looks great in his white dress uniform. The admiral will have his aide to attend him, and Durand will attend the admiral's wife."

"That would be Hatpin Harriet?" I said with a grin.

"Yes, sir. You know she got that callsign one night at the Saenger Theatre downtown during the intermission of *The King and I*. The crowd at the ladies' room entrance wasn't moving fast enough for her, so she took a hatpin from her hat, yelled, 'Out of my way; I'm the admiral's wife,' and jabbed the woman in front of her, who jumped out of the way, allowing Hatpin to be the next through the door. I don't envy Jesse, but he gets a little extra duty pay for putting up with her, so he's okay with it. That guy's always finding ways to make extra money."

We turned onto the wide concrete area between the last two hangars and stopped. With their two-story sliding doors closed, they both looked abandoned.

"This is the hangar, Mr. Lewis," Pete said as he pointed to the fourth hangar. I don't think these last two have been used regularly since Korea.

"I don't see anyone around. How do we get in?"

"There's a pedestrian door at each end beside the large hangar door."

"Hope it's not locked."

The heavy steel door squeaked and moaned when I opened it, which may or may not have alerted the man who hollered at us from behind. We turned. A sailor in denim trousers, a denim sailor cap, and a soiled denim shirt with three red stripes on the sleeves jogged toward us and jabbed his finger at us.

"Where are you going?" the sailor said.

I reached for my wallet and blocked Pete to remind him that I was to do the talking. The sailor stopped before me.

"Good afternoon, sir," I said. "My name is Dan Lewis, and I'm with the State of Alabama aircraft accident investigation team." I flashed my gold North Carolina detective's badge. "As the accident—the Cadet Puckett accident—happened on civilian property, I've been sent here today to ensure that the aircraft involved in the accident has been properly secured and remains available to us for further study. I met this cadet where I parked my car and talked him into being my escort."

"Does my chief know you're here?"

"I don't know, but I assume so as the gate guard passed me through."

"Oh, well, still, I'd better go in there with you. It's been off limits to all personnel."

"So, no one has been in to see the aircraft?"

"I saw an officer go in there right after it was dropped off, but I believe he was part of the aircraft recovery team. No one since then except the Navy accident investigators."

"Hey, Stink!" The voice came from across the concrete. Another sailor in denim stood in the entrance to the opposite hangar and held the door open. "Your wife's on the phone!"

"Ah, crap," the sailor said. "Hold on. I'll be right back." He jogged away.

"Scoot," I said as I opened the steel door to more creaks and moans. "I'll meet you back at your barracks."

"But?"

"You're talking orders, remember? I've got to keep you out of this, and I've got to get in there before that sailor has a chance to call the gate guard."

Pete did an impressive about-face and marched off toward the street.

I eased the door closed behind me and stared into the dark pit of the hangar—a dank, musty, oily smell hung in the air. Shadowy forms of a dozen or more wrecked aircraft, like an aircraft graveyard, appeared packed in the back of the hangar. As my eyes adjusted to what little light came through the dirty windows along the top of the hangar doors, I noticed one aircraft standing near the doors and in one piece—a T-28 with muddy tires.

I jogged over to the T-28, climbed onto its left wing, and examined it inside and out. I found a large hole in its left side, damage to the panel on the right side of the cockpit where the male plug from his headset was still plugged in, and blood everywhere, but something that should have been there wasn't.

CHAPTER 10
The Reticent Pathologist

With Pete back in his barracks and the denim sailor none the wiser about me, I returned to Pensacola and stopped at Carl's legal office. There, the well-kept, gray-haired woman in gold handed me two fresh notes.

I smiled, thanked her, and walked to the phone on the table by the entrance. I read the notes and then called Carl's office.

"Hey, Carl. Dan. I'm downstairs and just got your note."

"Yeah, Red. Look, ah, I've got some bad news. I just found out that you're off the case."

"What?"

"Yeah, Cliff, my senior partner, told me to call you in. He says Pete is off the hook now, and Jeff's death is an accident, and—"

"Whoa, Carl. Hold up. I'm not so sure it was an accident. It may look that way, but until I've seen the coroner's report, I'm proceeding with a murder investigation, and I'm expecting to be paid as you promised. Remember? You said, 'You're on the payroll, Dan.' So, I expect a paycheck at the end of the week."

"I know, Red, I know, but Cliff calls the shots here, so I'm sorry, but you're off the case."

"So, no payday?"

"No, but pay through today, and all your expenses covered, including the hotel and return train fare."

"And rental car?"

"Through today. Turn it in first thing in the morning. Have National send us the bill. And if you'll turn in your expense report first thing tomorrow, we'll pay that."

"Geez, Carl. I didn't see this coming, but if that's the way you want it…"

"It's not me, man; it's Cliff. I'm sorry. Are you still going to the reception tonight?"

"I guess so. I have a note to call Miss Jones so she may back out."

"Well, whether I see you tonight or not, I'll take you to the train tomorrow afternoon."

I hung up. After a few seconds of dwelling on the fact that I'd been fired twice in less than three days and was once again unemployed, I shook it off and called J.J. at her newspaper. She picked up immediately.

"Hey, Dan. Thanks for calling back."

"Sure. What's up?"

"I've learned that Flood will not be at the reception tonight but will see us this afternoon. Can you be available at four? I'll pick you up."

"You bet. Did he mention the coroner's report?"

"He just said he wanted to go over the case with me. Your appearance will be a surprise."

"Oooo-kay."

"Not to worry," she said with a chuckle. "He knows who you are."

I waited for J.J. at 3:55 in front of the San Carlos. She arrived at 3:56 in her red Ford sedan and drove us to the Naval Air Station Pensacola. We went through the visitor's pass procedures and proceeded to building 600, Mustin Hall, the Visiting Officer's Quarters.

Lieutenant Flood met us in the lobby, which featured a centered, large crystal chandelier from the ten-foot ceiling, a marble floor, and leather furniture on both sides. On the right side was a wide fireplace. A large oil painting of a vintage naval seaplane hung over the mantle, giving the lobby a nautical touch.

Flood's height, weight, and gangly build brought Ichabod Crane of "Sleepy Hollow" to mind, but the look belied his confident handshake and erect posture. Even my surprise appearance didn't seem to phase him. At his invitation, we sat on stuffed leather chairs around an oval coffee table in front of the fireplace.

He adjusted his round wire-rimmed glasses, then patted his chest through his navy-blue uniform blouse with gold, anchor-embossed buttons.

"In the file I have inside my blouse," Flood said, "is a copy of everything I compiled when planning for the defense of Cadet Dalton in the Cadet Puckett accident case, including the coroner's report, which I found very interesting. As the Navy has declared this a civilian-caused accident and absolved itself of any culpability, I have orders to move on to other things. I think that's a mistake, but orders are orders."

J.J. leaned forward like she wanted to speak, but Flood held up his hand.

"Miss Jones, there is information in here I'm sure you'll want to report in your paper, but remember, if you want the Navy's cooperation ever again, you'd better clear anything you write with the base Public Affairs Officer. I believe you know Commander Oxley. He's not someone you want to cross, so please heed my advice. You can only report what he approves. And if you ever want *my* cooperation again, you will never mention my name as the source of this information. Agreed?"

"I understand, Lieutenant, and I agree," J.J. said. "But why are you doing this?" She glanced around the lobby. "Why take this chance of angering the command?"

"I'm naïve enough to believe in justice, Miss Jones, and blaming this case on a farmer with a rowdy dog and a quick trigger finger doesn't pass the smell test for me. You'll understand once you read through the information in the file."

Flood cleared his throat. "I see you brought the large purse I requested."

"I did," J.J. said as she patted her patent leather shoulder bag.

"Good. Now, let's walk to the restrooms down the hall," Flood said as he nodded to the hallway behind us. "I'll give you the file as you enter the ladies' room, then I'll continue to the men's room. When you exit the restroom, have the file in your purse, pick Mr. Lewis up in the lobby, and depart."

A few minutes later, back in the car and on Moffett Road, I asked to see the file.

"In due time, Dan. Right now, I've got to get home and dress for the reception. You're still going with me, right?"

"If I see that file."

"Okay, okay." She handed me her purse. "But read it to me as you read it."

"Ah, I'm not going to read it in the car, at least not while it's moving."

"What?" she said, turning onto Murray Road and heading for the main gate.

"I don't like to read in the car, that's all."

"Ah, bull! You get carsick, don't cha?"

"I don't like to read in the car. At the next traffic light, I'll take a look."

"Na-nana-naa-nah." She bounced up and down on her end of the bench seat like a three-year-old. "Mister tough-guy detective gets carrr-sick."

"J.J., grow up. Pull over here at this warehouse, and I'll read the file to you."

She pulled over, grinning all the time, and stopped. Meanwhile, with the car idling, I opened the file, flipped through the paperwork and photos, and found the coroner's report. I scanned it and focused on the bottom line.

"Well?" J.J. said.

"Well, it's just as I suspected and as Lieutenant Flood hinted at."

"Well, well?"

"It concludes that Cadet Puckett died of respiratory failure caused by the trauma of the crash and a massive loss of blood from a gunshot wound, a GSW."

"Boring. We knew that. At least we knew the GSW part. What's with the respiratory failure?" She pulled back onto Murray Road.

"Yeah, that doesn't fit for me, and I'm sure it didn't fit for Flood. What's missing here is a toxicology report. That might explain the respiratory failure better than stress and blood loss."

"So, they didn't do a toxicology report?"

"They either didn't do one, or they did one and didn't like the results."

"And buried it?"

"And buried it."

"Who signed that report, Dan? Who did the autopsy? Navy or civilian?"

"Commander Lester Amick, MD," I said after we had stopped at a traffic light and I had a chance to refer back to the file. "Know him?"

"Never heard of him."

"Maybe he'll be at the reception. Hope so, but I also hope to get a chance to speak with Cadet Jesse Durand. He was the number three guy in that gunnery flight. He'll be there escorting the admiral's wife."

"Oh, yeah—Hatpin Harriet," she scoffed. Then she scrunched up her face in a puzzled look. "Dan...this toxicology thing...surely Scotty McTavish's lawyer...what's his name? Do you know?"

"Ernest Applewait is the name I've heard."

"Oh, yeah: 'Juice' Applewait. Retired Navy."

"Really?"

"Yeah, I did a story on him, oh, months ago. Interesting guy. Flew seaplanes in World War Two, cargo in Korea, then retired as a Lieutenant Commander and went to law school. Very gung-ho Navy retiree. Very inexperienced defense attorney."

"Then why would Mr. McTavish hire him."

She took a hand off the wheel and rubbed her fingers together.

"Oh, yeah," I said. "Scotty, the Scot, got a deal."

"That would be my guess. But surely even Juice Applewait would want a toxicology report."

"Unless he could get his client off with a slap on the wrist—say a small fine for accidentally hitting Jeff's airplane—then he may not want to open that toxicology can of worms and risk a black eye for his precious Navy. For example, if Jeff was on some kind of dangerous drug, prescription or otherwise, that's not good advertising for your NAVCAD program."

"Well, you know the family. Could he have been on drugs?" She drove out the main gate, then turned right onto Barrancas Avenue.

"With Jeff, anything was possible, but I can't see it. By all accounts, he was doing well in the program and loved it. And he was healthy; no cold or anything that would suggest he was taking over-the-counter medicine that would have caused respiratory failure. Plus, drugs are not the kind of trouble he's been into before. No history of that."

"What about caffeine? Those guys live on coffee. Can you overdose on caffeine?"

"Oh, sure, in very high doses, but those side effects aren't fatal. At least, not right away. Look, J.J.," I said as I closed the file, "we're pushed for time now, so let me study this after the reception. Then return it to you later tonight."

"That sounds good. And stay for a nightcap? How about that?"

"Oh, well, we'll see. If it's not too late."

At six o'clock, I arrived to pick up J.J. in my navy blue sports coat, blue and red striped college tie, and gray slacks. She exited the elevator in a long, white cocktail dress with a V-neck and gold waistband highlighting an hourglass figure and a buxom cleavage. A gold clutch-style purse completed the look. I had to look again to make sure it was her.

"Yes, it's me, Dan." She stopped and posed in the first position. "You approve?"

"Well, yeah. Absolutely."

"Do I look grown up now?"

"Very."

"Good." She took my arm. "Back to the base, please, sir."

At all the old military bases I'd been to in my Army career, like Fort Benning, Georgia, and Fort Bragg, North Carolina, I'd always been impressed with the sturdy, mostly Greek-classic buildings that served as quarters, clubs, and even education spaces. Mustin Beach Officer's Club at N.A.S. Pensacola was the same and an excellent example of Greek symmetry, pediments over entrances, and tall double doors below arched transoms. Along with the manicured grounds, the club seemed to stand for tradition, strength, and crisp military bearing."

At the cul-de-sac at the end of the drive, I parked along the curb and in front of the arched blue awning that allowed a shaded and dry entrance to the club's columned porch.

"I'll park and be right back," I said as I opened the passenger door for J.J.

"See you inside," she said.

A cadet in his dress-white uniform held a door for her, and I drove around to park.

On my walk back to the entrance, a couple, including a large woman and a slender gentleman with a lot of gold on his epaulets and the bill of his cap, stepped from a black Cadillac staff car. The car flew blue flags with four white stars from its front fenders, and another officer in white held the car door.

I entered the club a minute later and found J.J. outside the ladies' room on the right side of the expansive foyer. She chatted with the same large woman who had exited the staff car, and that woman looked familiar, including the Mamie Eisenhower hairdo with a squashed hat and veil.

"There you are," J.J. said to me. "I want you to meet Mrs. Cushenberry, the admiral's wife. She's heard about you, Dan."

"Oh?" I said. Mrs. Cushenberry offered her hand, so I took it. "My pleasure, Mrs. Cushenberry."

"Yes, I have heard about you, Mister Lewis. From North Carolina, I believe."

"That's correct. Sand Hills. A good golfing community if you play the game."

"Do you play the game, Mr. Lewis?"

"I don't play that game, but I do play board games, like Clue. I like murder mysteries."

"Indeed. Murder mysteries. Is that why you're in Pensacola?"

"Mrs. Cushenberry, if you know who I am, you must know why I'm in Pensacola. Oh, and please call me Dan."

"Touché, Dan." She smiled and turned to J.J. "He's charming, J.J. Thank you for introducing us." She nodded to the tall cadet waiting for her by the opening to a spacious main room that teemed with people drinking, smoking, and talking over loud music. I saw the cadet glance at me before he turned to offer his arm to Mrs. Cushenberry.

"That's Cadet Durand, isn't it?" J.J. said. "He knows you, I could tell."

"Yes, Jesse Durand. He was dash three in Jeff's flight of four on the day of the accident."

"Have you talked with him?"

"Not yet," I said.

"I have, briefly. Last month, I tried to write a story

about him. You know, the first negro NAVCAD and all, but he wanted no part of it. Even when the command pressured him, he said no. Very private young man but impressive. Worked his way through Ohio State." She hooked her arm on mine. "Shall we join the madding crowd?"

"Yes, and while we're among that madding crowd, keep your eyes peeled for a commander with the medical insignia on his uniform. That's the guy I want to talk with."

"Deal, but first check this out: The admiral's daughter, Teri, with a new beau." She nodded toward the open double doors to the bar on our right, where a stunning young woman with long red hair slinked out of the bar on the arm of a chiseled Navy lieutenant. Each carried a half-full martini glass.

"And wouldn't you know it," she added. "It's Tom Hornsby, who is twelve years her senior."

"You know Hornsby?" I said as I stopped and looked her in the eye.

"Knew him well."

"How well?"

"Well enough to have been engaged to him."

"What? Really?"

"Yeah, really." She scoffed. "I wonder what momma Hatpin thinks of this development?"

"Isn't Teri just seventeen?"

"Eighteen this week, but going on twenty-one. Smokes, drinks, and is every bit as bossy as her momma. If Hornsby is dating her without being ordered to, he's not thinking with the head that's on his shoulders."

"Yeah. Ah, look, J.J.," I said as Hornsby and Teri slinked through the crowd without noticing us, "can I get you a drink?"

"Sure, double scotch. Rocks. I'll meet you by the fireplace. I see someone I need to talk with."

At the crowded bar, I slipped in between two Navy officers in white uniforms with their backs to me and waited to get the attention of the closest of the two bartenders, the short, dark one with the Filipino accent. The two officers beside me nursed a cocktail and focused their attention and conversation on the officer facing them. By the time I had a chance to place my order, I was captivated by the conversation on my right that included a war story of a guy who had been shot down in Korea, bailed out, and then had to climb a tree to be rescued by the ship's helicopter.

When the other guy in the conversation said, "That's nothing. I was—," one of the two guys on my left said to his guy, "That's it, doc. I've got to get back to my woman. Hope your flight back to Jacksonville goes well." That got my attention.

I turned as the guy departed and left me facing a short, overweight Navy commander with the silver acorn on top of a spread oak leaf on the collar of his white short-sleeve uniform shirt.

"You're a doctor?" I said.

"Yes, but I'm a pathologist first and a medical doctor second. Name's Amick."

"I'm Dan Lewis, Dr. Amick. Nice to meet you." We shook hands. "So, you're Commander Lester Amick?"

"Yeah. Do I know you?"

"Oh, no, Commander, you don't know me, but I know you by your work on the Cadet Puckett accident case."

"Really?" He straightened.

"Yes, sir. As a pathologist, you did the toxicology report on the deceased, didn't you?"

"Yes, but—"

"And you would have made that report available to the accused's legal team, right?"

"Yes, if necessary, but look here, Mister Lewis, that's Navy business, which means it's none of your business."

"Oh, but it is my business, Commander. Cadet Jeff Puckett was a friend of mine."

"Excuse me." He plopped his tall cocktail glass on the bar and turned for the main room.

"Ah, sir," the bartender with the Filipino accent said. "Your drinks, sir. That'll be a dollar."

I gave him a five-dollar bill and watched the doctor head into the main room toward Hatpin Harriet.

When the bartender returned with my change, there was a note under the one-dollar bills. "See me later," it said. "I have info." I looked up, but he ignored me. I left a dollar on the bar, pocketed the three dollars and note, and walked toward the main room.

CHAPTER 11
The Autopsy

I found J.J. leaning against the back of a fabric-covered sofa, conversing with a distinguished gray-haired civilian in a blue suit and tie. I sipped my beer, handed her the scotch, and introduced myself to the man.

"Ah, J.J.," the man said, shaking my hand and looking up at me. "Your friend is a tall one." He cracked a conspiratorial smile. "And a sudden addition to the guest list like me, are you?"

"Yes, sir, very sudden, and it doesn't seem to be going over well with some." I looked across the room, where the doctor and Hatpin stood by the other fireplace sitting area, watching me. Carl and Caroline Puckett sat on the sofa behind them in conversation with the man with the gold epaulets.

"Dan," J.J. said, holding out her hand to the gentleman, "this is Arnold Lentz, President Emeritus of *The Pen-*

sacola News. I've been telling him about the work you've been doing on the Puckett case, and he's impressed."

"Indeed I am," Lentz said. "How would you like to work for the *News*, Mr. Lewis?"

"J.J. told you that I'm a detective, right? Not a reporter or a photographer."

"Well, yes, she did," he said, "but a reporter is just a detective who can write, and even if you're not Ernest Hemingway, we have editors and rewrite people who can polish your report."

"I'm flattered, Mr. Lentz, I really am, but this is kinda sudden. Let me think about it. When do you need an answer?"

"Oh, later tomorrow would be okay." He looked at J.J. "Could you take him under your wing tomorrow, J.J.?"

"I could take him under my wing tonight if he's willing." She winked at me.

I paused for a second to make sure I'd heard her correctly and then said, "I'll let you know tomorrow, Mr. Lentz. And thank you for the offer."

A glance to check on the Doctor Amick and Hatpin conversation was in time to see Jesse Durand slip through the crowd and head our way.

"Join me," Jesse said under his breath as he walked past me and continued toward the bar.

"Mr. Lentz," I said. "your hands are empty. Let me get you a drink. What'll you have?"

"Nothing for me, Dan. Doctor's orders."

"Not even a ginger ale?"

"No, only water for me these days."

"Then water it is. Rocks?"

"Yes." He grinned. "Water on the rocks."

"J.J.?" I said.

"I'm good, Dan." She took a sip of her scotch.

"Okay then, I'll be right back." I set my half-empty beer glass on the marble fireplace mantle and turned for the bar.

At the far end of the bar, by the windows darkened by nightfall and out of sight of Hatpin, I slid in beside Jesse just as the Caucasian bartender with a high-and-tight haircut handed him a martini with an onion and olive.

"Admiral's tab?" the bartender said.

"Yes, sir," Jesse said.

"For you, sir?" he said, looking at me.

"A Bud on tap, please."

"What's up?" I said as the bartender moved to the center of the bar and out of hearing range.

"You're Dan Lewis?" he said in a solemn tone with a solemn look.

"Correct."

"Pete told me about you. I only have a second, but I think somebody—didn't see who—slipped something into Jeff's coffee while we were in the ready room before Jeff's accident."

"A drug?"

"Not sure, but I remember Jeff saying that his coffee didn't taste right, so he added more sugar and topped off his cup. I thought he meant it wasn't hot enough, but looking back on the sloppy way he flew that flight, I think something was in that cup besides coffee and sugar. Either that or someone might have drugged his cigarettes. Meet me at Abe's 506 Club on Belmont tonight if you want to talk about it." He picked up the martini and hustled off.

I kept my back to the exit, gave Jesse time to get into the main room, and then looked around for the Filipino bartender. He wasn't there.

I joined J.J. and Mr. Lentz in time to see the admiral and Hatpin take a position behind a podium on the side of the room opposite the entrance. Jesse held Hatpin's drink and stood off to the side. The admiral's aide stood off on the other side. A young Navy captain and a beautiful blonde, presumably his wife, stood behind them. After introductions and glowing comments from the admiral, the captain made a short speech. The crowd applauded and returned to the hors d'oeuvre table and punch bowl.

That's when I realized the Filipino bartender was serving the hor d'oeuvres. He picked up an empty tray and returned through the entry to the bar on the other side of the fireplace.

A few minutes later, J.J. and I had just said our good-byes to the departing Mr. Lentz when a light hand tapped my shoulder, and a whiff of "Evening in Paris" washed over me. I turned to face Carl and Caroline.

"Hi, Dan," Caroline said with one of her sorority-rush smiles, then she hugged me gently, properly, while she kissed the air by my cheek.

"Hi, Caroline." I extended my hand to Carl. "Carl."

"Red." Carl glanced down like a guy who had just had the keys to his car taken away.

"Ah, Dan," Caroline said as she took my arm and turned me away from J.J. and Carl, "can we talk?"

"Sure, Caroline, darlin'." I looked back at J.J. and said, "Excuse us, please. We'll just be a minute."

"This may take more than a minute, Dan," Caroline said as we walked away, and she leaned into me like a conspirator.

"No, it won't, Caroline. I don't want to neglect my date, you understand. You do understand, don't you?"

She cleared her throat. "Dan, please. I know we haven't been best friends, but I was hoping you could appreciate our position. I hate that Cliff has let you go before we even had a chance to get you out to the house for dinner, but it's for the best."

"How? How is it for the best, Caroline?"

"Well, you knew Jeff." She stopped and faced me. "We loved him, of course, Dan; everybody loved him, but he wasn't good for the family. He was a distraction, if you will; his trouble with the admiral's daughter and all, and with Carl running for office, it just wasn't a good time for him to be on the scene. This town is full of Navy people, Dan. They follow the admiral's lead, and we need their votes."

"So, you're glad Jeff's dead?"

"Oh, certainly not, but what's done is done, and the sooner the story dies, the better."

"Is that why Cliff sacked me?"

"Oh, no, Dan, I'm sure that's not it, but you need to be back at your job in Sand Mountain—"

"It's Sand Hills."

"Oh, of course, Sandy Hills. But I'm sure they want you back there as soon as possible, and Cliff thought you'd done all you could do here, so he did what he thought was best."

"What he thought was best, or what *you* thought was best?"

"Oh, please, Dan." She held her hands to her chest as if in prayer. "Please don't think I had anything to do with this, but please just accept our thanks for coming and return home."

"Caroline." I braced and pointed at her. "I'll return home when I finish this case. Get that through your

pampered brain, and don't suggest leaving to me again."
I took her by the arm. "A minute is up."

We found J.J. and Carl still conversing by the fire-place.

"Let's go, Carl," Caroline said when we stopped.

"Let me finish my drink, darlin'. Miss Jones was telling me a fascinating story."

"I said, let's go, Carl." She took his arm and led him toward the exit. Carl handed me his cocktail glass as he passed.

"Well," J.J. said as Carl and Caroline disappeared in the crowd that moved toward the foyer, "that was fun."

"She wanted me to give it up," I said after I sipped my fresh beer.

"The case?"

"Yeah. Said pursuing the case and keeping it in the papers was bad for Carl's campaign. Or words to that effect."

"Boy, that apple didn't fall far from Dad's tree."

"No, it didn't, but speaking of politics. I think it's time you got in touch with Uncle Walker. We need that toxicology report now more than ever."

"Oh, you learned something?"

"Yeah. There's a good possibility someone drugged Jeff's coffee in the ready room that morning."

"So, that could explain the respiratory failure?"

"Depending on the drug, yes. We need that report to identify the drug."

"Home, James, and I'll make the call. But first, give me a minute to interview the new skipper of the *Saipan*. I've got to have that story in tonight for tomorrow morning's paper."

"That's fine. I've got to see a bartender."

I got J.J. home at eight and then returned to the San Carlos to call Connie and to study the autopsy report.

"Hey, Connie, it's me."

"Hi, 'Me,' I've got news for you."

"About the chief? He's okay, I hope."

"No, about Fort Bragg. The chief is still in ICU. No change."

"Humm. Sorry to hear that. Okay, what's the Fort Bragg news?"

"Bullock found the Fort Bragg moonshiner, and you were right; it's a she."

"Great. Is she in custody? If so, where?"

"No, she's dead."

"What?"

"Yeah, stabbed. Looks like somebody got to her before she could be arrested."

"Humm. Well, if you can rule out a relationship problem, then I'll bet it was someone who didn't know about the arrest warrant. Someone threatened by her sales success, maybe."

"You mean someone like the Heisters? Looper and the boys?"

"That's where I'd look first."

"Okay, we're on it. What's new with you?"

"Well, let's see…I've been fired again, but the plot thickens on the case, so I'm not leaving just yet."

"But if you've been fired…"

"But I've also been hired."

"What? Ah, come on, Detective Lewis, explain yourself."

"They want me to be a reporter for *The Pensacola News*. Can you dig that? Me a reporter?"

"And just who is 'they'?"

"Oh, the president emeritus of the *News*."

"I'll bet that was Miss Jamie Lynn Jones' idea."

"She may have suggested it, but Mr. Lentz, the president, made the offer."

"So, you're not coming home?"

"Not yet. But soon. Unless the Navy throws me in the brig."

"That's a possibility?"

"No, just kidding, but I have the impression they don't want me to continue on this case, so we'll see. Say, how's Nate?"

"He's fine. He's still eavesdropping for you, determined to find out who killed the moonshiner woman."

"Tell him I said hello. And now I have to study an autopsy. Good night, Connie."

"Nite, Dan. Oh, and I'll tell Becky hello for you, also."

"Oh, yeah, okay."

"And don't forget to eat right. And behave yourself. Promise?"

"Yes, ma'am."

I settled into a stuffed chair and poured over the autopsy pages and photos for the next thirty minutes, but nothing stood out as a smoking gun. So, without a toxicology report to question the doctor's findings, the autopsy conclusion that Jeff died of respiratory failure from blood loss and trauma would stand. At least I learned that Jeff suffered the facial trauma because he didn't lock his shoulder harness before he "crashed." And that explained Dr. Holmes' notes that he treated facial lacerations before Jeff expired.

I called J.J. and arrived at her apartment around ten o'clock. She met me at the door in "something comfortable," a silk nightgown robe featuring a fur collar and wristbands.

"Whew. You look great, J.J., but I've really got to get back. It's been another long day."

"Nonsense." She took the file from my hand. "Drag your butt in here, and let's talk about this case. For instance, why did you have to see a bartender?"

"Ah, yeah, the bartender. Well, he had some information for me about the case."

"Okay. Share, please." She sat on her green velvet two-cushion sofa and offered me the cushion next to her, but I took a club chair on the other side of the glass coffee table.

"Drink?" she said. "I picked up some Bud for you."

"Oh, gee, that was thoughtful, but no thanks. Not now. Well, back to the bartender. He didn't have the information himself; his friend had it and would talk with me tomorrow at lunch. In Foley."

"The friend is in Foley?"

"I guess."

"Can I go with you?"

"If you want to hitchhike with me."

"No rental car?"

"No, I've been fired by my friend Carl and his lovely, rich, and very political bride. She wants the Jeff case to disappear and me with it."

"Hey!" Her eyes lit up. "You've got to take the reporter job now."

"Looks that way."

"Great. You'll like being under my wing, Dan. It's soft and warm under there."

"I'm sure it is, but I'm not ready to be under anyone's wing right now. I'm ready for a good night's sleep." I stood. "Please look at that file, and let's compare notes tomorrow. I've got to turn in my convertible in the morning, so if you don't mind driving, we should leave here around ten."

"You're a hard case, Dan," she said with a dejected slump, then slapped her hands on her thighs and stood. "But I'm not giving up."

At the door, she hugged me and said, "Wish you'd change your mind and stay."

I didn't change my mind, but I jumped into a cold shower as soon as I got to my room at the San Carlos. Sometimes, it was really, really hard for me to "behave" myself, and that was one of those times, but duty called, and I still needed to see Jesse that night.

Refreshed, I dressed in my sports coat and tie again and headed to Abe's 506 Club. I'd never heard of that club and didn't know Belmont Street, but I'd check my map and find it. If Jesse Durand hung out there in the segregated city of Pensacola, it was bound to be an exciting place—probably the kind of place where you had to know someone to gain entry.

CHAPTER 12
The Mysterious Sailor

The sidewalks of Belmont and DeVilliers, crowded with colored folks, jumped with jazz music pouring from the windows and doors of Abe's 506 Club and the Savoy Ballroom. I drove carefully through the intersection and watched smiling men and women strut up and down the sidewalks; the men dressed in suits and ties with spit-shined shoes and fedoras, the women in short flashy dresses and heels, all feeling the music. A few looked at me suspiciously, but most smiled and waved as I passed in my golden glow yellow convertible with the white interior. I smiled and waved back but didn't see Jesse. I finally found a parking spot two blocks down Belmont.

When I returned to the club, Jesse waited outside the door with a petite young woman and a warm smile.

"You know, Mr. Lewis, your low and slow pass in that

convertible was a big hit," Jesse said with a chuckle. "Yes, sir, big hit. Especially with the women." He nodded to the young woman clinging to his arm. "And that included Vivian here, my fiancée. Viv, this is Mister Dan Lewis."

"Hello, Mister Lewis. Welcome to The Blocks," she said.

"Thank you, Vivian, but please, both of you, call me Dan. Okay?"

"Well…if you don't mind, sir," Jesse said. "I'd rather stay with Mister Lewis. My daddy taught me that if the man is older than you, he's a Mister and a Sir."

"I won't ask you to go against your teaching, Jesse, but I don't think I'm that much older than you."

"As my daddy would say, 'Older is older.'" He smiled that warm smile again. "So, what do you say, Mr. Lewis, would you like to go inside? You'll love it. Abe's has the best jazz and blues this side of New Orleans; Louis Armstrong, Fats Domino, and Ray Charles have all entertained here. No big names tonight, but the joint is still jumpin'."

"I'll go in if you think it's okay, but I don't want to impose."

"It's a small club, and they're a little jealous of their space, but it's okay if you're with us, and we'll just stay 'til the end of this first set. I want to talk with you at some point, and it'll be hard to talk in there."

"Then let's go." I made a little white-guy dance move, and that cracked them up.

From our standing-room-only space against the back wall, I bought a round, enjoying the jazz licks and watching people have a good time, and I also enjoyed receiving the same respect I gave them. A good memory, but it ended too soon, and then we walked outside. I checked my watch.

"Geez, Jesse," I said. "It's after eleven."

"Yes, sir, I know, and I've got an early class tomorrow." He pointed. "Let's walk to the bench on the corner and talk. Then I've got to get Viv home and split."

When we reached the corner, Vivian sat while Jesse and I stood by the streetlight.

"Mr. Lewis, Jeff's accident wasn't an accident. Someone had it in for him."

"That's my conclusion as well. Who do you have in mind."

"Okay, it had to be somebody in the ready room with access to Jeff's coffee. Jeff owed Dusty money, so even though Dusty didn't like Jeff, it didn't make sense that he would kill him. He'd never get his money that way, so I'd rule him out."

"Maybe Dusty just wanted to shake him up and show him how vulnerable he was, scare him into paying up," I said.

"Well, that could be, but whatever it was in that cup

was strong enough to kill the guy. That's a little beyond scaring him."

"I agree, Jesse, but unless Dusty's a pharmacist, he wouldn't know a scare dose from a lethal dose."

"He's definitely not a pharmacist," Jesse said and scoffed. "He treats everything with aspirin, even athlete's feet."

"Well, let's don't rule Dusty out yet. Who else was in that ready room?"

"Me, Pete, Jeff, of course, Hornsby, and the attendant."

"Attendant?"

"Yeah, a Filipino guy named Reyes. He prepares and serves the coffee and keeps the ashtrays cleaned out, and then he sweeps up at the end of the day and takes out the trash. Those guys come from the Philippines but are in the U.S. Navy and assigned jobs like the mess hall, the quarters, and ready rooms. They become citizens that way."

It occurred to me that Reyes might be the guy I was supposed to meet the next day for lunch in Foley, but I decided to keep that to myself for the time being.

"Reyes, huh?" I said. "What do you know about him?"

"Nothing. The guy's like a ghost. He comes and goes, but we hardly ever see him."

"Never talked with him?"

"No, sir. We only know his name because it's stenciled on his denim uniform shirt."

"So, you've never seen him interact with Jeff?"

"Oh, well, Jeff called him back into the ready room and yelled at him one time because the coffee wasn't hot enough. And he did it in a demeaning way, like some white folks do to colored folks. But that was it, and that was one of the few times we actually saw the guy."

"Speaking of demeaning treatment, have you had any trouble?"

"With other cadets or instructors? No, sir. Well, one instructor clearly wasn't happy to see a negro in the program, but I never had to fly with him. It's been some of the enlisted colored guys who have given me the cold shoulder and called me things under their breath. But just a few."

"I'm glad to hear that. Now, at the reception, you mentioned Jeff's cigarettes. You still think that's a possibility?"

"Heck, I don't know. I don't smoke, but it could work, couldn't it? I mean, it had to be in something he consumed, so that's either coffee or cigarettes."

"I don't smoke either, but I've heard of spiking cigarettes to poison someone." I grinned. "Not in my professional life, but maybe on a TV show. Still, it might work in real life. I'll see if I can access his personal effects and check it out."

"To me, it had to be something he consumed in the ready room without knowing it."

"Agreed, but if it was in his cigarettes, somebody could have done that the night before. Wasn't he drunk, and didn't Teri have to sneak him back onto the base in the trunk of her car?"

"Yeah, that's right. So, anyone could have gotten to his cigarettes while he was asleep in our room."

"Possibly, yes. Now, how about Pete? Can we rule him out?"

"Yes, sir, Pete's a good guy. I'd rule him out."

"How about Hornsby?"

"Oh, yeah, Hornsby. Tough on everybody. Hard to please. Spring loaded to the pissed-off position, as we say. He didn't like anybody, but he does like girls. Big womanizer. And a show-off. Did you know he has an airplane? A yellow N3N, also known as the 'Yellow Peril.' He gets his kicks by taking girls up in that airplane, scaring them with loops and spins over the Gulf."

"N3N. Open-cockpit biplane, right?"

"Yes, sir. Old World War Two Navy trainer. It's kinda like a Stearman but not a Stearman."

"So, Hornsby's a show-off and a womanizer but wasn't a threat to Jeff."

"No, sir. Wouldn't think so. Hornsby treated all of us the same—badly."

"So, we're down to Reyes or Dusty with no real motive for either."

"Yes, sir, and before you ask, the morning of the accident, Jeff overslept again, so he went from his rack to his clothes to the ready room. He didn't even shave or brush his teeth, so there wasn't an opportunity for him to get that drug from anywhere other than coffee or cigarettes."

"If he was drugged."

"He was drugged, Mister Lewis. There's no doubt in my military mind."

"I know you've got to go, Jesse, but one more question: Think back to that gunnery flight, from the ready room activity to taxi for takeoff. Did you see anything or notice anything unusual during that time?"

"No, I...well, yes, sir. On the flight line. I'd finished my preflight, strapped on my parachute, and climbed onto the wing when I saw Hornsby put his parachute on the left wing of Jeff's airplane. Then he threw Jeff's parachute over his shoulder and walked off."

"Where was Jeff?"

"On the other side of the airplane doing the starboard side preflight."

"So, Jeff didn't see the swap."

"I don't know, but if he did, he probably didn't think anything of it. Jeff could have picked up Hornsby's parachute by mistake in the paraloft. I mean, he's done it before, and Hornsby was swapping to get his back. If that's all, Mister Lewis, we've got to make tracks. Thanks for coming."

"That's it. Good night, you two." I shook hands with Jesse, then offered my hand to Vivian. She took it and popped off the bench.

"Good night, Mr. Lewis," Vivian said and made my white-guy dance move, which cracked us up again; then she gave me a quick hug. I still get a chuckle when I think about that.

The next morning, under a sky thick with dark clouds and a spring rain that pounded my convertible top, I returned the rental and walked back to the San Carlos under a San Carlos umbrella. Carl waited for me in the restaurant.

"Hey, Red," Carl said sheepishly as I sat at our table by the window. "I could have picked you up at the rental place."

"Morning, Carl. When you didn't offer it on the phone, I decided I needed the exercise. Did you bring Jeff's effects like I asked?"

"Ah, no. Caroline thought we should hang on to them for a while."

"Caroline thought, huh? Hey, Carl, ol' buddy, do you ever think for yourself anymore?"

"Well, sure, but Caroline is the one with the political instincts, and she doesn't want you poking around Jeff's personal effects."

"I wonder why. Were there cigarettes among his effects?"

"I guess so."

"What do you mean, you guess so? You haven't seen them? He was *your* brother."

"Yeah, but Caroline picked up his stuff, and she said there was nothing there. Just a wallet, some change, and his class ring."

"He was a smoker, so wouldn't you figure there would be cigarettes and a lighter? And if she didn't mention those items, didn't you wonder why?"

"Well, no, I didn't. But why would you wonder why? What are you driving at?"

"He may have been drugged, Carl. That's what I'm driving at, and the drug may have been in his cigarettes."

"Oh."

Carl stared at his coffee. Then he looked up, and I watched the lights come on in his hen-pecked brain. His eyes widened, and his jaw dropped.

"Red! The sloppy flying, the fall out of formation, then safely landing the airplane, then the respiratory failure! That was drug-induced?"

"Could be, but we'll need the cigarettes so we can have them tested."

"Yeah, yeah, but are you sure he was drugged, and are you sure it was the cigarettes? I mean, if he was drugged, couldn't he have been drugged another way?"

"*If* he was drugged, and I believe he was, it could have been in his coffee, but that evidence disappeared in last Friday's trash. So, to rule that in and cigarettes out, we need the cigarettes."

"Then…, Red, you're saying he was murdered."

"He was probably drugged, but that may or may not have been with intent to kill, so murder maybe, but hopefully not."

"Here." He handed me his menu. "Order for us, and I'll be right back." He stood. "I'm calling Caroline."

When Carl returned to our table, our slender, middle-aged waitress, dressed in black and a little white apron, smiled, took our order, and warmed our coffee.

"Well?" I said, reaching for my coffee as Carl sat.

"She said she told the Navy to throw them away."

"Great."

"I'm sorry, Red, really. I know Caroline can be a pill sometimes, but she means well."

"She means to get you elected at any cost, Carl. That's what she means."

We finished our breakfast in silence, and then Carl asked if I wanted him to take me to his office to close out my expense account. I said yes. Then he asked if I wanted him to take me to the train depot that afternoon. I said no. When he asked if I'd checked out of the hotel, I said no again, and then we left for his office. At least he picked up the check.

The rain stopped around nine o'clock. J.J. arrived at nine-fifty-five wearing white clam-digger pants and a blue and white striped blouse tied at her tanned waist. I gotta admit I took a second look.

On our way to Foley, just before we got to the Lillian Bridge over Perdido Bay, we passed the expansive, two-story Paradise Beach Hotel set back among tall pines on a circular drive called Paradise Beach Circle.

"That's where Hornsby keeps his girlfriends when they're in town," J.J. said, pointing at the hotel. "Took me a while to figure that out. It's a little run-down now, but it was quite the hot spot for parties and dances in its day, the big band era. Some big names played there: Dorsey, Goodman. Got a beautiful little beach on Perdido Bay behind it."

"His girlfriends?" I said as we got to the Lillian Bridge.

"Yeah, I don't know if they were for him or if he was playing matchmaker for his students, but they would come in from towns in the area, usually mill towns, and I guess they were looking for a Navy pilot husband, him or someone else. Anyhow, I got tired of it and tired of him."

I heard the roar of a piston engine airplane and looked out my window and behind us.

"Well, speak of the devil," she said, looking up through the windshield as a yellow biplane passed a few hundred feet above us in a shallow turn.

"Your fiancé?"

"My *former* fiancé," she said with a smirk. "He keeps that airplane at Ferguson Field and plays around with it on his days off. He must not be on the flight schedule today."

"Ferguson Field?"

"Yeah, Ferguson's a civilian field a few miles behind us."

"Is that a redhead in the front cockpit?" I said, still following the flight of the N3N, which seemed to be moving in slow motion in the turn.

"Probably Teri, a future former fiancée. If it's her, Hornsby is in over his head. There's no future in dating an almost eighteen-year-old who is the daughter of a man who can ruin your life if you ever do something that girl, or that girl's momma, doesn't like."

"Did Jeff Puckett ever do anything that girl's momma didn't like?"

"Oh, yeah," she said with raised eyebrows. "One of my N.A.S. informers told me Puckett climbed into Teri's second-story bedroom window one night last week, convinced her to go drinking with him, then brought her back drunk and disheveled with a cut lip."

"You're kidding."

"Nope. Then Teri went to get him at Barin the next night, Thursday night, and they partied at some honky-tonk in Turkey Branch, Alabama, until late. That time, she had to sneak him back to his barracks in the trunk of her car."

"Oh, yeah. I've heard about that."

"So, good luck, Lieutenant Hornsby. Fly away, dark soul, fly away."

We rolled into downtown Foley at eleven o'clock and parked by the train station on East Laurel. I got out and stood by the car so I could be recognized.

"Where are you meeting this guy?" She said through the open car door window.

"The note just said eleven o'clock in Foley. I assumed that would be the train station."

"There's a couple of sailors," she said, pointing up the sidewalk to the corner of McKenzie Street and Laurel. "He's a sailor, right?"

"I assume so, but he might be a Filipino sailor."

"I don't see anyone like that."

"Me neither, but let's just cool it for a few minutes and give him a chance to find us."

"You cool it. I'm getting hot in this car, so I'm going to the corner under that live oak and sit on that shaded bench."

"Go ahead," I said as I looked up the street to the east toward Barin. "He may be waiting for me to be alone anyhow."

Ten minutes later, after I checked the depot waiting room, a train from the south stopped at the train station, and several sailors came out of nowhere and got on board, including a couple of Filipinos, but neither showed an interest in me. Finally, at eleven-thirty, I walked over to where J.J. was sitting and joined her on the bench.

"J.J.," I said, "looks like my guy's a no-show. I've got an errand to run, so let me do that, then let's have lunch." I pointed. "See the Foley Coffee Shop across the street?"

"Yeah."

"I'll meet you there."

"Great. I hope they've got ceiling fans. It's hot out here."

"They do. Tell Miss Lilly I sent you."

On the other side of McKenzie Street, J.J. went north to the Coffee Shop, and I continued west on Laurel to Manning Jewelry. It was time to see Betsy McTavish about that bracelet.

CHAPTER 13
The Little Brown Bottle

On my way to Manning Jewelry, I ran into the tall, blonde nurse Amy Anderson in her white uniform and cap coming out of Stacey's Drugs. She carried a little white bag and threw out her arms when she saw me.

"Oh, Dan," she said, "you've come to see me again. I love it!"

"Well, I am glad to see you again, Amy, but I'm actually headed for Manning Jewelry."

"Oh, that's sweet; you're gonna buy something for me, a little token of your affection."

"Ah, well, no, not exactly."

"Ah, shucks, Dan." She hugged me. "I'm just jerkin' your little chain, honey. You know I prefer short, strong lumberjacks."

"Oh, yeah, I remember that. And I've seen your Dusty. That boy could swing an ax alright; broad shoulders."

"Got that right," she said as she led me into the shade under the awning of a Foley Hotel window, "But that poor boy has been in distress lately. Did I tell you that?"

"No, don't think so. What's bothering him?"

"Well, he loved that gunnery flying, but now he's in the carrier qualification phase, and he's been dreading that for weeks." She leaned over to me. "He's afraid of landing on that itty-bitty aircraft carrier."

"He wanted to be a Navy pilot, but he's afraid of landing on an aircraft carrier?"

"Well, he wanted to fly, but the Air Force didn't want him, so…"

"Huh. But the Navy has land-based airplanes, too, you know."

"They do, but Dusty wants fighters, so I've been helping him out."

"How's that."

"Phenobarbital," she said as she held up the little white bag.

"Phenobarbital? That's a pretty strong sedative, isn't it?"

"That boy had been so worried about carrier qualification that he couldn't sleep, Dan. So, I gave him a bottle of this PB from our sample cabinet, and it's helped him a lot. I figure once he's relaxed and does the C.Q., he'll be over it."

"C.Q.?"

"Carrier Qualification. Come on, Danny Boy, do I have to teach you everything?"

"Probably," I said with a chuckle. "But I'm getting there."

"Good. Now, I've got to git, but come see me again, and I'll give you another lesson in flight school lingo, okay?" She hugged me. "And soon, you big ol' hunk of detective."

Amy walked to the hospital, and I walked to Manning, where I found Betsy with a female customer in a pink floral dress and a floppy hat. I stopped at the counter before Mr. Manning as he arranged gold chains on a velvet pad. He looked up, and I explained my financial setback and asked for my deposit on the bracelet.

"I understand," Mr. Manning said with a pleasant smile. "Be right back."

"Hello, Mr. Lewis," Betsy said as her customer left the store. She walked along the back of the counter to stop before me.

"Hey, Betsy. You have a chipper smile this morning."

"Well, thank you. Yes, things are going well. Daddy's home—"

"And Pete's called again?"

"Uh-huh. Just a minute ago," she said with a bit of blush on her cheeks.

"Good. Glad to hear it. Any news? About the accident or the guys he's flying with?"

"No, they're all doing okay, I guess. Their attendant is gone; that's new."

"The ready room attendant? Reyes?"

"Pete just said the Navy's transferred their little Filipino guy, and now they have a new guy who is a motor-mouth." She chuckled. "Which normally wouldn't be a problem, but they can't understand his pidgin English."

"Oh, I guess that could be a problem."

Mr. Manning walked up with my money, and Betsy noticed.

"Oh, Mister Lewis, you won't get the bracelet?"

"No, Betsy," I said as I took the money. "Not right now. Maybe another time."

"Ah, that's too bad. She would have loved it."

"I know."

"Well, look, you seem a little down, so why don't you join Pete and me tonight at the dog track? We'll show you around. Pete knows the dogs pretty good, so maybe he can help you win some money, and you can buy that bracelet. How 'bout it?"

"I appreciate it, Betsy, but…"

"Ah, come on. We'll pick you up. Where are you staying?"

"I'm at the San Carlos, but that's downtown Pensacola."

"The dog track is on this side of Pensacola, but it's still Pensacola, so no problem. How about eight o'clock?"

"Shouldn't we check with Pete first?"

"Sure, but he'll want you to come." She bounced a pointed finger at me. "Let's do this: I'll check with Pete, and if there's a problem, I'll leave a note for you at the San Carlos. Otherwise, we'll see you at eight. Agreed?"

"Okay, agreed." I nodded to Mr. Manning. "Good day, and thanks."

After a short walk in the hot sun, I entered the Coffee Shop and found J.J. in a booth with two sailors in denim shirts. The one on the end with the high-and-tight haircut had his elbows on the table, head in his hands, and eyes on J.J. like a cat looking through a fishmonger's window at the "catch of the day." And he looked familiar.

"Ah, there you are!" J.J. said, scooting over to the wall as I sat. "Gentlemen, this is Dan Lewis from North Carolina. Dan, this is Waco and Sniffles." She elbowed me. "They're with the Barin Field Crash Crew, and Waco works as a bartender in the evening." She elbowed me again. "At the Mustin Beach O-Club."

Waco slid his elbows off the table, looked up, and offered his hand.

"Sorry," Sniffles said as he held back and wiped his nose on a paper napkin. "Tree pollen, ragweed, whatever."

"I think I recognize you, Mr. Lewis," Waco said. "Were you at the reception last night?"

"Yes, and you poured a beer for me."

"Bud on tap. Yes, sir, I remember. That was some crowd, huh?"

"Sure was. Lots of interesting people, including that pathologist from Jacksonville."

"Oh, yes, sir, 'Mister Black Russian.' That's what he was drinking."

"Did you catch any of his conversations?"

"Did I eavesdrop? Of course I did, Mister Lewis; that's the best part of bartending. Well, that and the tips, but yeah, that guy bragged the whole time about how well he knew the admiral and the politicians at the reception. Apparently, he did some autopsy job for them. Big 'Yay me' kinda guy."

"What did he say about the autopsy?" J.J. said as she elbowed me again.

"Nothing in particular. He just made it sound like the job was a favor to either the admiral or the admiral's wife."

"The wife, huh?" J.J. said. "Hmm."

"Say, Waco," I said, "who was the other bartender last night? Filipino guy."

"Yeah, Teo. He works at the mess hall here at Barin, but, like me, he makes a little extra money at night tending bar and working in the kitchen at Mustin Beach."

"Does he have any close friends at Barin?"

"Oh, sure. Those Filipino guys stick together, but I

think Reyes is the one he mostly hung out with. They're from the same village or island or something like that."

"Have you seen Reyes lately?"

"Yes, sir. He was in town this morning, but I think he's been transferred 'cause he and his buddy were in dress whites and caught the train."

"Caught the train? Rats. I was supposed to meet him here."

"Oh, you're the guy!" Waco reached into his shirt pocket and pulled out an envelope. "Here, this is for you."

"From Reyes?"

"Yes, sir. He was in here about eleven and told me about meeting someone, but he seemed real nervous about being seen with whoever it was, so he gave me this, and said, 'He big guy. Red hair.' Then he left." Waco handed me the envelope.

"Well, rats again. I got a note to meet him in Foley, but it didn't say where, so I assumed it was the train depot." I put the envelope in my pocket.

"We think of Foley as this Coffee Shop. They give us a discount on lunch, and we hang out here a lot." He held out his hand toward Miss Lilly as she approached. "And we like to harass Miss Lilly."

"You don't know, harass, Mr. Waco. I know harass, and dat's what you gonna git if you don't order somethin' soon." Then she looked at me. "You again. Why ain't you in your office over dere." She pointed at the booth in front of us.

"I'm with this lady, Miss Lilly, and she got here first."

"Hubba hubba," she said, looking at J.J., then back at me. "You lucky man."

"Thank you," J.J. said.

"Now, folks." Miss Lilly put her pencil to her order pad, "Let's get on with dis. I got other customers, so order."

After lunch and walking east on Laurel to J.J.'s car, I pointed to a flight of two T-28s flying over the town toward Barin Field.

"Formation flight," J.J. said. "That comes after familiarization flights, basic instruments, acrobatics, and solos."

"And before gunnery," I presume.

"Correct."

Before we got to the car, I stopped under the live oak on the corner and opened the envelope from Reyes. J.J. stopped beside me.

"Hey, get this," I said. "Reyes saw a cadet pour something from a little brown bottle into Jeff's coffee *after* he, Reyes, had poured something from a little brown bottle into Jeff's coffee."

"What?"

"Yeah, says, 'I sorry, but I ordered. Not know it hurt cadet.'"

"Okay, but who ordered him to do it?"

"Doesn't say, but if it was an order, it must have come from an officer. I don't think Reyes would take an order like that from a cadet."

"You thinking Hornsby?" she said. "No, he might date the admiral's daughter to please the admiral or the admiral's wife, but he wouldn't drug somebody to please them."

"Maybe someone higher than that. Someone in command of the Filipino sailors."

"Or someone in command of the guy in command of the Filipino sailors. Like the admiral," she said.

"The admiral? Geez, J.J., you think the admiral would do something like that?"

"If Hatpin told him to, yes. Lowly Cadet Jeff Puckett had crossed her, remember? He'd messed with her precious spoiled brat daughter. And the admiral wouldn't have to order it himself. All he'd have to do is tell his aide that he wanted Cadet Puckett to fail his last gunnery flight or that he didn't want Cadet Puckett to graduate. It's called 'C.O.'s wishes.' If the Commanding Officer, or C.O., in this case, the admiral, wanted something to happen, he would only have to let those under him know what he wanted. When it happens as he 'wished,' and it goes wrong, the admiral is not at fault because he didn't give an order."

"So, the aide decides to drug Jeff through Reyes to please the admiral, so—"

"Well." She held up her hand. "Maybe. It may or may not have been the aide. It could have been someone else who had the power to give an order like that. Also, the admiral may have been thinking that the word would get to Jeff's instructor that the admiral wanted Jeff out of the program, so the instructor would simply fail Jeff. The drugging idea probably came from whoever didn't want to deal directly with Hornsby, who can be, shall we say, abrasive, but he thought that sloppy flying would get Jeff a failing grade, which would get him out of the program and please the admiral. I'm sure they didn't plan to kill him."

"You're sure, huh?" I said.

"Yeah, I'm sure, but somebody decided to drug Jeff, so they ordered the guy in charge of the Filipinos to get it done, and that guy ordered Reyes to do it, then they transferred Reyes so he couldn't be questioned."

"Then a cadet, probably Dusty Rhoades, topped it with a dose of phenobarbital."

"What?" she said.

"Yeah, I ran into Dusty's girlfriend on the sidewalk a few minutes ago. She's a nurse, and she gave Dusty a bottle of phenobarbital to calm him at night and help him sleep. Dusty had a grudge against Jeff, so he could have dosed Jeff's coffee to make him look bad."

"Dusty was the cadet Reyes saw?"

"He's the most likely, and I know he had the means, the phenobarbital."

"But there's still the question of that first dose from Reyes. What was it, and where did it come from?" J.J. fanned herself with a folding fan from her purse. "God, it's hot today. Let's get on the road."

When we were back in the car, I said, "I think I know how to find out where that second dose came from. By the way, have you called Uncle Walker yet? We've got to see that toxicology report."

"My friend," J.J. said as she started the car, "have I got a surprise for you."

"Okay. Surprise me."

"In the glove box before you is a telegram I got from Uncle Walker this morning."

"Oh? That's good. I hope. Is it?"

"Read it and see for yourself. I called good ol' Uncle Walker this morning and picked up his telegram just before I came to pick you up."

I retrieved the telegram, which lay on top of a beavertail blackjack, or *sap* as the criminal element called it.

"Say, J.J., what's with the blackjack?"

"Personal defense. Hornsby has one, and he gave me this one for Valentine's. Yeah, Valentine's." She grabbed herself over her heart. "Gets you right here, doesn't it?

True love." She sighed. "But it's practical; a girl has to be careful these days, you know." She started the car.

"Careful? Geez. I'm hangin' out with Miss Armed and Dangerous."

"Ha," she laughed. "A blackjack's not lethal; you know that. Well, I guess it could be, but not in my hands. But in your case, you don't have to sweat it. Heck, I'd be pleased if you tried something." She batted her eyes at me. "You know that, don't you?"

"I'm taking the fifth on that one. Okay, let's see what Uncle had to say."

I opened the telegram and read, "See Lieutenant Emil Zackman, M.D., at N.A.S. dispensary. Expecting you today. Has copy of toxicology report for you."

"Wow," I said as I looked up. "That's service."

"Yep. If there *is* a toxicology report." She backed out of the parking spot.

"Oh, there is. I'd say this telegram confirms it, but just in case Doctor Zackman is humoring the Senator and making false claims, I know the pathologist did a toxicology report because he unconsciously admitted it to me last night at the o-club bar."

"Then, next stop, N.A.S. Pensacola," she said as she pointed the car east and gunned it.

CHAPTER 14
The Death

J.J. parked her red Ford in the shade of a live oak, and then we walked across the asphalt toward a white wooden building. A white sign with blue letters above the front veranda read, "N.A.S. Pensacola Dispensary." On the walk, with J.J. fanning herself, we passed an up-front parking spot with a racing-green Jaguar. A sign before the Jag read, "Lieutenant Zackman, M.D."

"At least we caught him at work," J.J. said as she pointed to the car.

"Where else would he be at one-thirty?"

"Oh, anywhere: Post exchange, service station, gym, barber shop, golf course."

"Golf course?"

"Oh, yeah. They have a beautiful golf course on the base, and you know doctors; they love to ride around in those little golf carts and chase those little white balls."

"Sounds like you've dated one of those, too."

"I've dated two of those, too." She took the wooden steps to the porch, and I followed.

Inside, a Navy nurse receptionist sat behind a desk with a bored look, a wrinkled face, and a fingernail file. A lit cigarette lay in the ashtray groove on her desk.

"Excuse me," J.J. said to the nurse. "We'd like to see Dr. Zackman, please."

"Got an appointment?" she said as she filed her nails.

"No, this is not a medical call. I'm Jamie Lynn Jones, and this is Dan Lewis. We're here to talk with the doctor about the Cadet Puckett accident."

"Is he expecting you, Miss Jones?"

"Yes, he is expecting us today. And now we're here."

"What time was he expecting you?"

J.J. looked at me, and I could see the fire building in her eyes. Then she leaned over the desk and into the nurse's face.

"To-day! That's what time he is expecting us. Now, will you let him know we're here, or do I have to search this shack until I find him?"

"Well, I never," the nurse sputtered. "No, you can't see him now. He's not here."

"So, who owns the Jag in his parking space? You?"

"His car is here?"

"Well, hello there," a man's voice said from the hallway.

We turned as a tall, young man with a cigarette in one hand and a putter in the other walked out of the hall. Dressed in a white polo shirt with a PGA logo and saddle oxford shoes, he carried his putter like a swagger stick.

"I'm back, Rachel," Mr. PGA said to the nurse. "Is my one o'clock ready?"

"Yes, sir, Doctor Zack. He's in room two. And prepped. Oh, and there's a walk-in in four—chemical burns. Grace is caring for him, but he'll need to see you."

"Very good. And who are these people?"

"I'm Jamie Lynn Jones, Doctor, Senator Wiremann's niece, and this is my friend Detective Dan Lewis of North Carolina. My uncle said you would be expecting us today."

"Senator? He looked at the nurse. "Senator?"

"Senator Wiremann," the nurse said. "Captain Albright called this morning. Talked with you. Very important. Toxicology report."

"Oh, yeah!" He thumped his forehead with the butt of his hand, and cigarette ashes flew into his wavy brown hair. "The toxicology report, of course. Yeah, It's in a file in my office. Come on in, folks, follow me."

He snuffed his cigarette out in the ashtray on the nurse's desk, and then he brushed the ashes from his hair as we walked down the hall.

When he entered his office, he dropped the putter into a black golf bag with a nametag that read in gold,

"The Zack Attack." While I admired his office, which looked like the office of the golf pro at Augusta National, he walked to a battleship-gray four-drawer file cabinet next to the window behind a large desk. Framed photos of himself with other golfers shared wall space with several diplomas and covered the side wall. Golf trophies filled the bookcase shelves. He opened the top drawer of the file cabinet and yanked out a file.

"Have a seat, Miss Jones. It is Miss, isn't it?" he said with his best devilish grin while giving J.J. the same once-over Waco gave her in the Coffee Shop.

"Ah, yes, it is, doctor," J.J. said with a toss of her shoulder-length hair.

I didn't hear her suggest he could call her J.J., so that told me she would stick to business, at least for the time being. We sat in sturdy wooden chairs in front of the doctor's desk.

"May I see the file now?" J.J. said.

"Oh, well, see the file, no. The Captain just told me to show you the toxicology report." He smiled. "I'm sorry. Orders, you know." He removed a sheet from the file and handed it to her.

J.J. scanned the report and then handed it to me.

"Whoa, Miss Jones." The doctor pointed to the report in my hand. "Take it back, please. My orders are to let *you* read it, not your friend, Mister Lewis."

"Doctor, your orders will include Mister Lewis if I call my uncle. May I use your phone?"

"Ah, they would, huh? Hold on." He threw a switch on the intercom box on his desk. "Rachel, get the captain on the line for me, please. Stat."

"Right away, doctor."

I handed the report back to J.J.

"Doctor," J.J. said. "This report seemed to suggest that Cadet Puckett was drunk. Is that correct?"

"Oh, yeah, well, not drunk per se, but his blood alcohol level was right at the legal limit." He cracked a smile. "The boy was probably out partying the night before."

"And was that a contributing factor to his accident?" J.J. said.

"Contributing, maybe, but not the key factor. At least not the way I read that report."

"Captain Albright is on line one, doctor," Nurse Rachel said on the intercom.

"Excuse me, folks." The doctor picked up the receiver from the phone on his desk.

"Lieutenant Zackman. Yes, sir...yes, sir...yes, sir, I understand. I'll do that." He hung up.

"Well?" J.J. said.

"Well, I'll have a copy of the report typed for you, Miss Jones, and then you and Detective Lewis can take it with you. How about that?"

"That would be wonderful, Doctor Zackman. Thank you."

"But, Miss Jones, I understand you're a reporter, so we must insist that you will not report any of the information in this toxicology report in your newspaper or anywhere else. We have to agree on that."

"Oh, of course. I agree."

"Excellent. Then, if you and Mr. Lewis will wait in the lobby, I'll have this for you in a few minutes."

He called Nurse Rachel on the intercom, and we left for the lobby.

More than ten minutes later, Nurse Rachel returned to the lobby with a manila envelope and handed it to J.J. without comment.

Back in the car, under the shade of the oak tree, J.J. opened the envelope and removed a single sheet of paper. She turned it so I could see it.

"Note the blanks," she said.

"Looks like they're playing hide and seek with us, J.J. Let me look." I took the sheet from her and scanned it.

"The alcohol findings are still here," I said, "but as a contributing factor."

"Yeah, but I remember a whole paragraph about phenobarbital, and that's not here."

"And vomit and sweat-soaked clothing, which are symptoms of a sedative overdose. I don't see that in there now either, and it looks like they're going to stick with the same bottom line: death by respiratory failure from blood loss and trauma."

"Are you buyin' it?" She said.

"No, of course not. We saw the phenobarbital discussion that was in the original, so if Reyes had orders to drug Jeff, and we know he did, and then Dusty added his dose, the powers that be would certainly not want that known. But the original report didn't say the phenobarbital level was enough to be fatal—close, but not quite, so as bad as that could be if publicized, there still might be something else. And they're ashamed of whatever it is, or they wouldn't be playing games with us."

"I did see something else, but it was a chemical name I didn't recognize." She leaned over and pointed to the section where the paragraph about phenobarbital had been. "In here somewhere."

"I saw that too, and I think I know what it is or was, but I need to call a friend in Raleigh and get his opinion. Then the question is, if that was a factor, where did it come from? Cigarettes?"

"So," she said, "should I go back in there and kick their butts until they give me the full report, or should I call Uncle Walker again?"

"Let me call Raleigh first. Back to the hotel, please."

"Yes, sir. And I've got to get to my place, change clothes, and get to the office."

Emmett at the reception desk got my attention when

I crossed the San Carlos lobby and held up a message for me. I received it, thanked him, and took the stairs to my room.

"Call me," the message said. Signed, "Connie."

As the room and phone bill at the hotel were now on me, I called the Sand Hills Police Department collect.

"Connie, Dan," I said when she accepted the call.

"Oh, Dan, I wish you were here. I've got bad news, lots of bad news."

"Start with the worst. What's going on?"

"The chief died early this morning. Mary was with him, but neither of his two boys."

"But they're both in the Army, right?"

"One Army, one Marine, but both overseas. But, Dan, we need you back here. This town is basically unprotected now. We've already had a robbery at the drugstore, and that attempted bank holdup is still unsolved. Please come home."

"Ah, Connie, I want to, but I'm too close to closing this case. Another day or two should do it."

"Do you really owe Carl that much? Come on, Dan. You owe us something, don't you?"

"I was fired, remember."

"No, I mean the community, the people here, including me and Nate. And Becky. Well, maybe not Becky. We need you, Dan. I need you!" She sniffled, and I heard the rustle of tissue.

"Geez, Connie. No, I don't owe Carl that much. I don't owe him anything anymore, but I do owe something to Jeff." I sighed. "Look, get an officer from Pinehurst or Aberdeen until I get back, and I'll get back as soon as possible. Believe me, I can't wait to get out of here and back to you. Maybe tomorrow. Maybe Saturday. Hang in there, okay?"

"Okay." She sniffled again.

"When's the funeral?"

"Oh, I don't know. Probably Sunday, but I haven't heard. Too soon."

"Any news from my Chief Eavesdropper, Nate?"

"Oh, yeah." I heard Connie cover the phone and blow her nose. "Yeah, according to Nate's sources, Calvin Heister of the Heister moonshining family is a knife collector, so he's now Nate's number one suspect, and Nate figures Calvin wouldn't be able to part with the knife he used, so he'd still have it somewhere, probably in his truck."

"What kind of knife was it?"

"The coroner's report we got from the Army said it was a short, curved stabbing knife, probably a 'kukri' used by the Gurkhas from Nepal that served in the British Army. Nate wanted to search Calvin's truck the next time he saw it at the diner, but I squashed that idea."

"Good. Tell Nate I don't want him to act until I return. And I agree that if it were Calvin's knife, he would still have it."

"I'll tell him."

"Gotta go, Connie. I'll call again tomorrow. With good news, I hope."

"Bye, darlin'. Love you."

Then I called Sergeant Allen "Rat" Arrowood, the guy in Raleigh who attended the forensic class with me the year before. He was on the pistol range for annual firearms training, so I left a message and asked him to call me.

I sat at the desk in my room with my legal pad and wrote everything I could remember about that toxicology report, hoping my subconscious would fill in the blanks. I only recalled that the other chemical wasn't familiar, started with M, and had a toxic sound.

The phone rang at 4:10.

"Dan Lewis," I said.

"Yes, sir, Mister Lewis, this is Pete Dalton."

"Yeah, hi, Pete. Speak to me."

"Betsy suggested I call you. We were hoping you could meet us at the dog track this evening. They have half-priced beer on tap tonight, so all of us will be there: Dusty, Amy, Jesse, Viv, all of us. Betsy said she invited you."

"She sure did, but I wanted to make sure it fit your plans."

"Oh, sure it does. Looking forward to it. We'll show you around, maybe win some money, and drink a little cheap beer. How 'bout it?"

"Well, I could use another flight-student lingo lesson from Amy, so if I can bring someone, I'll be there. Eight o'clock?"

"Hey, got a date, huh? Excellent. Bring her along, and eight is good. We'll be in the lounge area."

"No, not a date. Just a friend with a car. I had to give up the rental. See you there." I hung up and called J.J. at the newspaper office.

"J.J., Dan. Can you talk?" I could hear typewriters banging away and voices from all sides.

"If it's quick. I have a deadline for this bridge expansion story, and I'm pushed for time."

"How about going to the dog track with me tonight? The guys in Jeff's flight and their girlfriends will be there. We might learn something."

"Oooh, a date with a tall detective."

"Now, now," I said with a chuckle. "This is business."

"Maybe for you, it's business, but I told you I wasn't giving up."

"So, you can go?"

"I can go, and I can go all night. What time?"

"Ah, okay, they want to meet us at eight."

"Then I'll pick you up at seven-forty."

"Sounds like you've been there."

"Oh, yeah. You-know-who took me there often, in fact, so often I began to think he had a gambling problem. See you at seven-forty."

At six, I sat in the restaurant with a menu all ready to order a grilled pompano when the waitress approached and told me I had a call. I thanked her and walked to the house phone by the phone booths.

"Dan Lewis," I said.

"Hey, Red, Allen in Raleigh."

"Ah, thanks for calling back, Allen."

"Ha, you didn't call me Rat this time, so you must want something."

"Okay, you got me. I need to pick your brain, Allen. You ready?"

"Pick away, but according to my wife, you won't find much there."

"Tell her she must be thinking of shopping brain cells, and those of us with the more dynamic XY chromosomes don't have much of those."

"Sure, I'll tell her that," he scoffed. "Then you can visit me in the hospital. Now, what's on your mind?"

"Okay. In that forensics class we took together last year, there was a lot of talk about everyday chemicals and how to recognize their use as a murder weapon. You remember that section?"

"Yep. I've had to use my notes from that class twice already. What's your question?"

"What do these symptoms and signs tell you? Erratic behavior, vomit, sweat-soaked clothing."

"Sedative overdose."

"Like phenobarbital?"

"Or something else in that class, but definitely phenobarbital."

"What else could it be?"

"Well, a pesticide would cause those symptoms. Something like malathion."

"That's it!—malathion, an odorless agricultural pesticide. But it only comes in liquid, right?"

"As far as I know, yes, only liquid."

"And there's a way to confirm it was the murder weapon, but I can't remember."

"I can't either, but I'll call you again if it's in my notes. Where are you, anyhow? This was a long-distance call, you sneak."

"Yeah, but I'll make it up to you. I'm in Pensacola, Florida, on a private case."

"Well, don't forget we have a job for you when you return."

"I haven't forgotten. Thanks, Allen. Appreciate it."

I called J.J. back and asked her to bring the file she got from Lieutenant Flood when she came to pick me up. The answer had to be in that file.

CHAPTER 15
The Showdown

For the first time, and probably for the first time in her life, J.J. arrived late.

"Sorry, Dan. I couldn't decide what to wear," she said from the car window.

"Well, you made the right choice," I said as I opened the passenger door and admired the black pants, black-and-white print collared blouse, and white sandals.

"Is that the file," I said as I sat.

"Yep, right here." She patted the file in the middle of the bench seat.

"Okay, let's roll. I'll look at it when we get there. Meanwhile, while we're with the guys, I'd like to find out where they're from, particularly if they came from a farm."

"Just ask them, you mean?"

"In a casual conversation, yes, but not directly. I don't want to arouse any suspicion."

"Where are you going with this?"

"I believe Jeff died of malathion poisoning, not phenobarbital. I know Jesse is from Mississippi, so he could have knowledge of malathion, and Dusty is from lumber country in Oregon, so he might know of malathion, but I don't know where Pete's from."

"Leave it to me. I'll find out."

J.J. followed 98 toward Alabama, then on the west side of Pensacola, she turned onto Dog Track Road. The track, brightly lit with light poles, glowed in front of the grandstands behind the parking lot.

After we parked, I flicked on the ceiling light in the car, opened the file, and took out the photographs. I flipped through them, examining each in turn, then put the close-up picture of Jeff's face on top and studied it, especially the eyes.

"That's it," I said as I tapped the photo.

"What's it," she said.

"Constricted pupils. Malathion. Things are finally making sense, J.J." I looked up and clicked off the light. "I don't know what Dusty put in Jeff's coffee, but whatever it was, even if it was phenobarbital, didn't kill him. Do you think Hornsby will be here tonight?"

"I know he's here." She pointed to the front row of

the parking lot. "That's his new Ford Thunderbird, the yellow one." She scoffed. "As in 'Yellow Peril.'"

"Good, that might work. J.J., just fly wingman for me tonight, okay? Cover my six, as the guys would say."

"Cover your six? What are you up to?"

"I'm on a mission, and I need a wingman. Will you do that for me?"

"I guess. But don't do anything stupid."

We took the stairs to the lounge and found the guys and their girlfriends in casual wear and seated at a table close to the track viewing area. Pete saw us first and waved.

"There goes Swifty!" suddenly blared from speakers on every pole supporting the roof of the lounge viewing area.

Everyone stood and faced the track except Pete. He motioned to us as he stood and pointed out two chairs beside him. We joined him in time to hear a bell ring and see seven colorfully attired dogs in leather muzzles leap out of their starting gates and chase a stuffed rabbit at the end of a steel pole. The pole was attached to a machine on tracks behind the inside fence. People around us, including Dusty and Amy, yelled at the dog of their choice, but Pete and Jesse just wore a calm, amused smile.

"I don't think they have a dog in this race," J.J. said, nodding at Pete and then Jesse.

"Apparently not," I said with my own amused smile.

Unlike horse races I'd been to, the dogs finished in less than a minute and probably closer to thirty seconds. A loud voice announced the winners over the loudspeakers, and Dusty screamed.

"Ladies and gentlemen, your attention, please," Dusty said to his friends. "I won the quinella!" Amy patted him on his back, and then he danced off toward a wired window with other winners.

I looked at J.J.

"Quinella," she whispered. "You pick two dogs to finish first and second in any order."

"Oh."

I held J.J.'s arm and said, "For those who don't know her, this is Jamie Lynn Jones of *the Pensacola News*. And J.J., this is Pistol Pete, Betsy, Jesse, who I think you know, Vivian, or 'Viv,' and Amy, my flight school lingo professor. That happy camper who just left is Dusty."

"Nice to meet all of you, and thanks for inviting us," J.J. said as we sat. "Where is everybody from?"

"Beautiful downtown, Foley, Alabama!" Amy said, "And Dusty's from Oregon."

"Ohio," Vivian said.

"Mississippi, then Ohio," Jesse said.

"Also, Foley," Betsy said.

"Texas," Pete said. "Dallas, Texas, where we learn to ride and shoot right after we learn to eat solid food." We laughed with him.

"I've heard you're the deadeye in this group, Pistol Pete," J.J. said. "Did you do your shooting on the farm?"

"We've all done well in gunnery, Miss Jones. No, I grew up on some acreage, so I had a place to shoot, but a family friend farmed our land, not us. I got into pistols because my uncle Clem owned a shooting range."

I stood. "That would explain your pistol range record, but hey, when's the next race? I want to try my luck, but first, I want to try a beer."

"About twenty minutes," Pete said, "but hang on— Dusty's buyin'."

"Hi, fellas," a man said after placing his hand on Pete's shoulder. I turned to see Lieutenant Hornsby's sun-tanned, rugged face.

"Welcome, sir," Pete said.

"Yes, welcome, Lieutenant," the others muttered.

"I hate to break in, guys, but I saw you with Detective Lewis and wanted to meet him." He looked down. "J.J., would you introduce us?"

"Sounds like that's unnecessary, Tom," J.J. said. "You seem to know him, and now he knows you."

"Dan Lewis, Lieutenant," I said as I offered my hand. "I've heard a lot about you from these young aviators and J.J."

J.J. stood. "Okay, now that that's over with, come on, Dan, I'll show you how to bet."

"Let me," Hornsby said as he pulled my chair out of

the way and stepped between J.J. and me. "This is my home track, Dan, so let's go. I'll show you how to win here."

I looked at J.J. She rolled her eyes and returned to her chair.

On our walk to the betting window, Hornsby handed me a race card and pointed to the second race, the one coming up, and the number 4 dog.

"I take it you've never bet the dogs before," he said.

"No, this is all new to me. Horses some, but not dogs."

"It's pretty much the same. My dog, the number four dog, is Yellow Peril."

"Your dog? As in, you own him, or that's the dog you're betting on?"

"I own him. J.J. doesn't know that. She thinks I called all those races she won because I'm lucky. I don't deny that I'm lucky, but I know how the game is played here and elsewhere."

We stopped short of the betting window and stood off to the side.

"Okay, Dan, here's the deal on this race. I have one of the two fastest dogs in the circuit this season. Now, Pensacola is the last stop for these dogs, so they're tired. I'm going to bet my dog to show, not win, so to make sure my dog is a little more tired than the rest, I've given him a little phenobarbital to slow him down. He'll finish second or third, and you'll make some money. You with me?"

"Phenobarbital, you said?"

"Yeah."

"Where did you get that? Prescription?"

"No, no, I don't need junk like that. Mrs. Cushenberry gave me some. She has a prescription."

"You and Hatpin Harriet, eh? Buddies?"

"Ha," he laughed. "Not buddies, but we understand each other. I help her, she helps me, and when she's at the track, she does remarkably well."

"I'll bet," I said with a chuckle.

"You'll bet now if you want to win some beer money; five dollars on number four in the second race to show. Just say that at the window. I'll do the same. As an owner, I can't bet against my dog, but I can bet for him."

When we returned to the table, Dusty handed out beers from a tray.

"Winner buys," Dusty said as he held up a beer for me.

Sure enough, Yellow Peril finished second in the second race, and my five-dollar bet paid twenty. From a seat on the rail overlooking the track, Hornsby turned and gave me a thumbs up. Then he pointed to the betting window and motioned for me to follow.

"I saw that," J.J. said. "Don't get suckered in by him, Dan. He's playing you."

"I know," I said as I stood and patted her shoulder. "Be right back."

In the third race, Hornsby said to bet on number 1. When I asked why, he said that number 2 tended to run wide in the turns and would force the fastest dog in the race, number 3, to run wider and take the other dogs with him, allowing number 1 a shorter route to the finish line. He said he could tell the starter had set up the race that way because people tend to bet on the fastest dog, so the track makes money when the fastest dog loses.

At the window, I bet on number 1 to show; he finished first, but I was in the money again.

"I guess I'm buyin' this time," I said to the guys. I turned for the cashier's window, and Dusty followed.

"Mister Lewis," Dusty said as we crossed the room. "I have a confession to make. I mean, I've *got* to make a confession. Amy insists. It's embarrassing, but Amy says you'll understand."

We stepped away from the crowd and stopped. Dusty glanced around.

"Okay," I said. "What's this confession all about?"

"In the ready room, before that last flight with Puckett…"

"Yeah?"

"Well, I didn't like the guy, right? He owed me money, and he wouldn't pay up. Even on payday, he refused to pay up."

"I've heard that, yeah."

"So, on that morning, in my bathroom, I pissed in a little brown bottle, then in the ready room before our fight, I poured it into his coffee." He looked down and scuffed the floor. "Childish, I know, but I did it, and I'm sorry."

"Dusty," I said with a smile, "based on the fighter pilots I've known, childish behavior is not just appreciated and approved; it's admired. You're gonna fit right in, son. Good luck."

I looked over at the cashier's window. Hornsby stood in line, so I patted Dusty on the back and joined Hornsby, who cashed in and then waited for me to do the same.

"Dan," he said as I left the window and walked toward the bar area.

"Hey, Tom. Got another tip for me?"

"No, I think you've got the hang of it now. I was just wondering if you've ever flown an airplane and, if so, what you thought of it. You know, was it fun for you."

"Flown in them, but never handled them. It might be fun, I guess, but probably not."

"Why do you say that?"

"Cause I get carsick."

"Ha, that's because you're not driving, man. You don't get carsick when you're behind the wheel, do you?"

"Well, no, I guess not. Good point."

"I tell you what. I have an airplane so easy to fly that

even Harriet Cushenberry could fly it." He chuckled. "Not that I'd ever give her the chance, but it's that easy. It's a slow and gentle bi-wing. How about going up with me in the morning when the air is calm? I'll teach you how to take off, climb, make some gentle turns, check out the beach, and return for a landing. What say?"

"Ah, man, I don't know. That's way out of my comfort zone. I was an Army military police type and much more comfortable on terra firma."

"But you won't know if you'll enjoy it until you try it. Believe me, I've taken some pretty skeptical people up before, and they all come back with a big grin and are eager to fly again.

"Tomorrow, huh?"

"Yeah. I'll meet you at Ferguson Field on Aeilron Drive."

"Ah, I don't know, Tom. Don't you have to fly at Barin tomorrow?"

"I'm on the afternoon schedule, so the morning is free. Come on."

"But I don't have a car."

"Have J.J. drive you. She doesn't go to the office until eight, and we'll be back by seven."

"Back by seven? When do we take off?"

"Six."

"Ah, no, that's way too early for me."

"Ah, hell, I'll pick you up. San Carlos, right? I'll be

there at five-thirty, and you better be ready. I'm gonna put you in that N3N, put a big smile on your face, and make you a believer in naval air."

"That's still too early. I'll be out late tonight."

"Yeah? With J.J.?"

"No, I've got to check on something." I paused. "Hey, maybe you could do me another favor. I know I'm pushin' it after you helped me win all this money, but you could be the answer to my prayers."

"I've had women tell me that a few times, but never a man," he said with a grin. "What do you need?"

"I need to get into Hangar Four at Barin."

"The graveyard hangar? What the hell for?"

"I think there's something in there that will prove Jeff Puckett didn't die of respiratory failure from blood loss and trauma. He didn't even die of phenobarbital poisoning."

"Now, wait a minute. You sure?"

"I'm as sure as I can be without seeing the inside of that hangar. Can you help? Can you get me in there tonight?"

"Well…" He looked at the floor and scratched behind his head. Then he raised. "No, Dan, I don't think that's a good idea."

"Ah, come on. We can be there and back in a little over an hour."

"It's that important, huh?"

"Yeah, it is."

"Oh, man, you're trouble, you know that?" He sighed. "Okay, let's go."

"Great. I'll tell J.J. we'll be right back."

We hopped into his Thunderbird, which still had that great new car smell, and hit the road. On our way, I checked the side-view mirror a few times, but I didn't see my wingman, that darn reporter who was supposed to be covering my six.

When we arrived, the Marine at the gate waved us through, and Hornsby drove straight to the line of hangars on the far side of the base, turned left, and parked in the lot across the street from number four.

"This is it," he said. "The graveyard."

"Is it locked?"

"Not usually. You still want to go in?"

"Well…" I glanced back toward the gate. No headlights. Quiet.

"Is it guarded?" I said.

"The Duty Officer will make his rounds later, generally after midnight, but guarded now—no, no guard."

"No guard, huh? Ah…"

"Look, Dan. You got me here to find something. Do you still want to find something or not?"

"Yeah, yeah, I do."

"Okay, let's go." He stepped out of the car and motioned for me to follow.

When we got to the pedestrian door on the corner of the hangar, lit only by moonlight through a broken layer of clouds, he stopped and slapped his forehead.

"Forgot a flashlight," he said. "Be right back."

The crescent moon disappeared behind the clouds, and Hornsby disappeared into the darkness. When I heard metallic noises at the car, I could tell he had opened the glove box. Then I heard it slam shut. He reappeared at the hangar with a chrome flashlight but didn't turn it on. I took that as a bad sign and glanced over my shoulder. Still no headlights.

Hornsby opened the steel door to squeaks and moans while I considered what he might do next. I had an inch of height over him and maybe a few pounds, but he looked hard as nails, and now he was armed with a flashlight with three D-cell batteries. I still thought I could take him if it came to that, but I wouldn't turn my back on him.

"Come on," he said, closing the door behind us.

I felt for and then flattened myself against the side of the metal stairs. He flicked the light on and shined it into the hangar bay—no T-28 with muddy tires.

"Okay, Dan. Where is this something?"

"I thought Puckett's T-twenty-eight would be in here."

"It was until this morning. Now maintenance has it in Hangar Two for a clean-up," he said as we walked to where it had been parked.

"Did they take his parachute with it?"

"Yeah, it was still in the seat pan."

"It was, huh?"

"Yeah, it was. What are you suggesting, Dan?"

"I'm suggesting it's still in here, and I figure it's hidden in one of those aircraft in the back."

"Yeah, well, you figured that, huh, Dan?" He chuckled as he shined the light in my face. "You know, I'd hoped you'd forget all this and go home. It's over, man. I mean, what's done is done, and you continuing to poke around is not good for anyone. It sure won't help Jeff. In fact, nothing could help Jeff. He was an accident looking for a place to happen and a danger to anyone in my Navy who had to depend on him. Besides that, the bum had it coming."

"Had it coming? How so?" I said, shielding my eyes from the light.

"I'm from North Carolina, too, Dan. A squalid little place called Rivertown outside of Charlotte. My father was a sharecropper on a cotton farm there, and the three of us—my father, me, and my little brother—plowed the field, planted the seeds, chopped the weeds, and picked the cotton. Then, my little brother, at age sixteen, fell in with a couple of thugs. One night, in an alley in Charlotte, they jumped a tall, redheaded guy and robbed him. Two friends came to the redhead's rescue. The youngest of the two friends picked up an empty whiskey bottle and cracked my brother's skull with it. But, you see… well, you probably know this…those bottles don't break like they do in the cowboy movies. My brother, Jimmy, is brain-damaged to this day. He's in a home that I support."

"Tom, I—"

"Shut up, Dan. I saw you slip into this hangar the other day. I figured it'd only be a matter of time before you got hold of that toxicology report, found the parachute I'd soaked with malathion, and put the puzzle together. Then I'd be charged with murder and be convicted, and then who would take care of Jimmy? My worthless father died years ago, and my mother left us years before that, so who?"

"But, Tom—"

"Shut up, Dan!"

Still trying to keep the light from hitting me directly in the eyes, I vaguely recognized him reaching behind his back and bringing out a revolver.

"This is a Navy issue thirty-eight revolver, Dan, and it's very effective at short range. Combat pilots carry them. I got this one in Korea. And now, here you are, trespassing on Navy property with this heavy flashlight, which will have your fingerprints on it. I saw the light and investigated, and you attacked me with the flashlight. Bang, you're dead."

"But there are so many holes in—"

"Oh, Dan, please shut up."

"You're hanging yourself, Tom! Listen! This show-down with the thirty-eight is cold-blooded, premeditated murder. That's not what you did with the malathion. The malathion might have soaked through Jeff's sweaty flight suit and caused respiratory failure, and maybe he would have crashed at sea and covered the evidence as you no doubt intended, but there were other circumstances—the phenobarbital, the gunshot—all of those factors added to the chances of a fatality, but you didn't have a hand in those. See? Killing me is only digging a grave for yourself."

"So what?" he said, raising the revolver and sighting in.

The gun fired as I squatted to the floor and scooped a handful of dirt where the tires of the T-28 had been. He sighted in again. I threw the dirt in his face. He dropped the flashlight and grabbed his eyes. I pounced, yanked the .38 away, and wrestled him to the floor. Then I heard a loud click and was blinded by dozens of lights from the hangar ceiling. Something warm ran down my neck.

"Mr. Lewis!"

CHAPTER 16
The Wrong Choice

As my eyes adjusted to the light, Jesse, Pete, and Dusty ran up and helped me pin Hornsby to the floor. Hornsby had blood all over him. I pressed my clean hand to my neck. Wet.

"Get the first aid kit by the stairs!" Jesse said as he turned. "Attached to the wall. Hurry."

I heard quick footsteps and looked to see Vivian stop at the entrance to the stairwell. I stood as Dusty took over for me, but I felt a wave of woozy.

"Take the laces out of his shoes," Pete said to Dusty. "Tie his hands."

Dusty sat on Hornsby, took off Hornsby's shoes, and removed the laces.

"You guys are gonna be sorry you got involved with this," Hornsby said with his face to a greasy spot on the concrete floor and hands behind his back. I'll see that none of you ever wear those gold wings. I have connections!"

"There's nothing here!" Vivian said and gestured back at Jesse in frustration. I see the panel where it was mounted, but the kit isn't there. It's gone!"

"Okay, okay," Jesse said as he pulled off his shirt. He folded it, moved my hand, and pressed his shirt to the side of my neck.

"Jesse, I'm okay," I said. "I'm bleeding, but I'm okay."

"You're darn right you're bleeding," Jesse said. "Come with us. As soon as we heard the shot, we sent Amy and Betsy to open the hospital, and we're going to get you there before you lose too much blood."

"Jesse's car is by the door," Pete said as he put my arm around his shoulder. "Let's go."

The steel door squealed, and two Marines entered the hangar with .45s drawn.

"Attempted murder," I said to them. "The weapon is on the floor near the perp, Lieutenant Hornsby, but don't mess up the prints." I wiped the blood from my hand on my jeans and removed my wallet. I showed my badge. "Arrest the Lieutenant and hold him. We'll be… we'll be…"

"Holmes Hospital," Pete said. "Come on, Mister Lewis. We've gotta hurry."

"Where's J.J.," I said as my vision darkened.

"Long story," Jesse said.

I didn't remember anything after that until I found myself on a hospital bed with an IV in my arm and Amy smiling over me.

"Hey," Amy said. "Welcome back."

"Holmes Hospital?" I said.

"Foley's finest."

"Foley's only," Betsy said from the foot of my bed.

"How bad is it?" I said.

"The bullet nicked your carotid artery, so you lost over two pints of blood, but Jesse and Pete are both type-Os like you, so they donated a pint each while Doctor Holmes sewed you up, so you'll be fine."

"But no more white-guy moves at Abe's for a while, Mr. Lewis," Vivian said with a chuckle. She leaned over from a chair on the other side of the bed and patted my shoulder.

"And Hornsby?" I said.

"On his way to mainside in the back of a car with bars in the windows and armed guards for company," Amy said. "The boys saw to that. They're downstairs."

"What should I tell them, Amy?" Betsy said as she turned for the stairs.

"Tell them he's fine, but don't be surprised if he wants to take up flying."

"Oh?" I said. "Why would I do that?"

"Well, sugar, now that you have flying in your blood, why wouldn't you?"

"Yeah," I said as I smiled with them, "and maybe I won't get carsick anymore." I raised a hand. "And Betsy, tell the guys I appreciate the rescue. Glad somebody had my six."

I felt weak again, but I asked Amy to call Connie collect at the home number in my notepad. Amy nodded and put another blanket on me.

"Enough talk," Amy said. "Sleep well. I'll be with you overnight, and the guys will see you tomorrow."

I woke up the following day in the same bed but in a different corner of the hospital with a pain in my neck. Sun from the west streamed through thin curtains in a window.

Pete sat by the window reading a manual and whispering words that sounded like he was memorizing procedures: "Speed brake, gear, wing flaps, cowl flaps, mixture rich, prop, hook, canopy."

"Hey, Pete, you got the Dan Lewis watch?"

"Yes, sir, my turn. How are you doing?" Pete said as he stood and placed the manual in his chair.

"I've felt better but don't remember when I've been thirstier."

"Got ya covered." He poured water from a metal pitcher into a glass.

"You guys aren't flying today?"

"Jesse and I gave you some blood last night, so we're

grounded for forty-eight hours. We weren't scheduled to fly our first F.C.L.P. flight until next week anyhow."

"You're speaking in tongues again. F.C.L.P.?"

"Field Carrier Landing Practice. We smash-and-dash, that is, we do touch-and-go landings at Barin for a week, then go to the carrier for the real thing. Can't wait." He handed me the glass and a pill. "Go easy on the water. Amy's orders. And take this pain pill."

"Thanks, and thanks for the blood. I mean, *seriously*, thanks for the blood." I took the glass from him, popped the pill, and sipped.

"Pete," I said as I held the glass on my chest, "what happened to J.J.? She was supposed to be covering my six."

"Miss Jones was playing for the other team, Mister Lewis. I mean, tell me, why would a good-looking woman like her, or any woman, go for a creep like Hornsby?"

"I used to think I knew, Pete, but now...well, maybe that's just one of those unsolvable mysteries...kinda like the Bermuda Triangle."

"Go figure, huh? Anyhow, after she watched you and Hornsby leave, she walked to the stairs, and I heard her mutter, 'That's not the plan.' So, I cornered her and reminded her that if anything happened to you, she would be an accessory. She finally confessed that the original plan was to take you flying in the morning, sap you with a blackjack, then dump you over the Gulf—an accident while you supposedly unstrapped and leaned out to take a picture."

"Ah, the 'Join me in the Yellow Peril' con." I took another sip of water.

"Yes, sir, but apparently, you had your own plan."

"I did. I needed to force Hornsby's hand and get a confession, but I chose the wrong wingman to cover me."

"Well, with her confession, and just in case Hornsby had a new plan that featured malice aforethought, we took off and set a new land speed record between Pensacola and Barin." He smiled. "It was great; a flight of two old cars hauling butt and doing tail chase at eighty miles an hour on Highway Ninety-Eight."

"And just in time," I said. "And hey, did anybody call Connie for me?"

"I took care of it for you, sugar," Amy said as she entered the room. "That woman loves you to pieces, Danny Boy. You better be good to her."

Amy stayed with me between patients the rest of the day, and the guys visited the next day. Even Carl came by, but I was ready to be released by then. Carl settled the hospital bill, took me to see Betsy at Manning, drove me to the San Carlos, settled my bill there, and then drove me to the train depot in time for the afternoon train. On the way, I told him the Hornsby story, and after that... well, I'd never seen Carl so humble.

"I'll take care of Jimmy," Carl said. "I'll find out where he is and take care of him."

Carl, who would become State Representative Carl Puckett, told me a week later that Hornsby, in a deal with the JAG prosecutor, admitted that the phenobarbital in Jeff's coffee had come from Mrs. Cushenberry, through Reyes' chief, when ordered by Mrs. Cushenberry and without the admiral's knowledge or his "wishes."

Lieutenant Hornsby received a dishonorable discharge and prison time for the murder of Cadet Puckett. I didn't press charges on an attempted murder charge, so he only did ten years in Leavenworth. Later, he returned to Florida, converted his N3N into a crop duster, and did well enough to resume care for his brother Jimmy.

Miss Jamie Lynn Jones received a fine and returned to Birmingham as a reporter for *The Birmingham News*.

All the guys got their wings and commissions, but only Pete and Jesse got fighters. Pistol Pete Dalton went on to fly the Navy's topline fighter, the F-8 Crusader. He didn't buy his red Corvette because he married Betsy, and as he said, "I couldn't afford both, but Betsy was just as hot as that car."

Jesse Durand formally married Vivian in the N.A.S. Pensacola Chapel the day he got his wings and commission, then confessed that they had been married since they graduated from Ohio State. NAVCADs were not allowed to be married, so they kept their marriage a secret for two years.

Dusty Rhoades went on to fly the A-1 Skyraider and flew 21 missions off the carrier USS *Ranger* early in the Vietnam War. He didn't marry until he left the Navy and returned to Oregon. Meanwhile, in 1959, Amy married a short, husky young doctor who moved to Foley after finishing his medical training in family practice.

I came home to Sand Hills and found a new office and job as Chief of Police. I also found Calvin Heister in our jail for the murder of the woman moonshiner, Slap Jack. And I discovered that Bullock had done a good job of collecting the kukri knife and other evidence that would get Heister convicted. That brought a smile. But I would still hire another officer, a woman whom Rat, err, Allen Arrowood, recommended. Connie would get her steak dinner at The Steak House and then be promoted to office manager, and Miss Jean Ann Tuley, blind but skilled, would be our new receptionist.

The best part of this story is that the diamond engagement ring I bought from Betsy with a thirty-day loan from Carl is now on Connie's finger, meaning Connie, Nate, and Becky—Heaven help me—would become my family. My brush with that bullet from Hornsby's .38 convinced me that life is too short to go it alone, especially if there's a woman you love who loves you and wants to go through it with you. Fortunately, I'd found such a woman in Connie, and I'd learned to use the word *love* without hesitation.

Epilogue

Connie and I married on the first of July that year. We had a perfect one-week honeymoon in the Smoky Mountains, then a personally difficult "bonding vacation" with Becky and Nate in Gulf Shores, Alabama. Because Nate and Superman found a girl's body on the Gulf Shores beach, Nate calls our resulting one-week investigation the case of *The Gulf Shores Murder*. Connie calls that week the case of *Becky's Belligerence*. With Nate getting help from a cute little blonde on horseback, I call it the case of *Nate's First Love*. Whatever the title, it was one heck of a week in the sleepy little community of Gulf Shores in the summer of 1956.

About the Author

Randolph Crew didn't start writing novels until he was in his fifties because, as he says, "I couldn't spell." He credits Word's spell check, a creative writing course at a junior college in 1990, and a great writer's group in Greenville, SC, as the path to his writing career.

In 1996, after four years of learning the craft and polishing his first manuscript, which was *A Killing Shadow*, a military action-adventure novel based on his Vietnam experience, he was told by literary agents that although his manuscript should be published and deserved to be published, it wouldn't be because it was about Vietnam and nobody cared. So, he self-published. He followed that in 2011 with a sequel titled *One-way Mission*. Both received outstanding reviews and high praise from those who mattered and from professional publications.

In 2016, Crew decided to have fun writing a series of cozy murder mysteries called *The Four Seasons Series*. This book, *The Barin Field Murder*, is Book 3 in that series, and Book 4 is *The Gulf Shores Murder*.

Crew is the proud father of a son who is a prolific reader and the proud grandfather of a granddaughter who is the number one fifth-grade reader in her school. He lives in Alabama and enjoys writing, speaking, and hiking in the great outdoors. You may contact him via the contact page on his website: www.rcrewauthor.com. He would love to hear from you.

Also, if you enjoyed *The Barin Field Murder*, please consider posting a short book review on Amazon. Thank you.

www.ingramcontent.com/pod-product-compliance
Lightning Source LLC
Chambersburg PA
CBHW030623120726
47904CB00006B/2009